# "VENGEANCE"

Vengeance
/ˈven.dʒəns/

the punishing of someone for
harming you or your friends or family,
or the wish for such punishment to happen.

## IAN KENT

Vengeance
Copyright © 2021 by Ian Kent

All rights reserved. No part of this publication may be reproduced, distributed, or transmitted in any form or by any means, including photocopying, recording, or other electronic or mechanical methods, without the prior written permission of the author, except in the case of brief quotations embodied in critical reviews and certain other non-commercial uses permitted by copyright law.

Tellwell Talent
www.tellwell.ca

ISBN
978-0-2288-5370-1 (Paperback)
978-0-2288-5371-8 (eBook)

# Dedication

To my lovely daughter Colleen, one of the brightest and most skilled people I know, (although she hasn't realized it yet). Colleen brought many of these problems to my attention, some of the main causes of global warming, how we are are paying too much attention to the petroleum industry and not enough attention to the animal agriculture, dairy and pharmaceutical industries.
Thank you Colleen, Love Dad

# Acknowledgements

As always, my deepest love and gratitude to my dear wife,
Diana for her support while I have my head buried
in my computer, for the many suggestions
and a lot of proof reading.

And . . . a real big thank you to my wonderful neighbour,
Jan Greenway, for her many hours of
meticulous proof reading,
grammar, structure, format, syntax and content suggestions.
Thank you, Jan!

# "Vengeance" Introduction

Global warming is a 'hot' subject in recent days (pardon the pun). Whether it is severe weather events, climate changes, glacier melting or sea level rise, they are all blamed on global warming. The main cause of global warming is a constant subject of debate, but fossil fuel usage receives the most blame, ie: the petroleum industry.

Recently, however, other contenders are rising to the position of blame for global warming, mainly the agriculture industry. Specifically, the animal agriculture and dairy industry. Animal agriculture has been accused of being the leading cause of climate change. Some estimates indicate that the production of animal based foods contribute almost seventy percent of total greenhouse gas emissions, whereas plant based foods contribute just over thirty percent. Other reports claim that Animal Agriculture methane emissions cause more global warming than all the CO2 emissions from fossil fuel sources.

Then there is the problem of land usage: according to the FAO, the United Nations Food and Agriculture Organization, livestock farming is the world's largest user of land resources, with grazing and croplands using almost 80% of all agricultural land.

In addition, water pollution is another unintended result of animal farming, including excess nutrients from nitrogen and phosphorus from fertilizers and animal excreta, pesticides, sediment and organic matter, pathogens, and drug residues and antibiotics.

Although these problems exist world-wide, many countries could be included as perpetrators of this problem, with the USA probably leading the world. Another cause for concern is the over use of antibiotics. In the USA, about 80% of all antibiotics manufactured are used in the animal farming industry. One would have to ask "How much of that is coming through on the meat I eat?"

Other environmental impacts stand out, like the water use of animal farming is staggering compared to plant growth. For instance, growing vegetables has a footprint of only 322 litres per kg., whereas pork uses 5,988 l/kg, and beef uses a massive amount of 15,415 l/kg.

This said, the problem not only exists in Canada and the USA, but throughout Europe, Africa, Asia and South America. Both Brazil and Argentina are huge animal farming countries, with the destruction of the Amazon rain forests of Brazil and other countries raising alarms. These forests are being cleared to provide more farmland for cattle or to grow grain to feed cattle. Considering the inefficiencies of that practice, one would question the wisdom of such a decision.

Many environmental organizations, activist and followers are descending on key cities in Argentina and Brazil to express their concerns, fight for what they think is right, and to oppose those in the agricultural industry who are not listening to the warning signs.

Of course, the industry is fighting back.

# "Vengeance" Prologue

Previously in the Jake Prescott trilogy:

Jake Prescott, a successful entrepreneur/scientist, had overcome many challenges during his lifetime, including losing his parents in a horrific car accident in Europe which left Jake with a bad leg, resulting with him using a cane. While at a major event during an environmental conference in Los Angeles where many people were killed, Jake and his staff get involved in an international manhunt for the perpetrators. With the help of Interpol and the FBI, they solve the mystery, but he loses his best friend and colleague, as well as his lover in a disastrous shoot-out at a chalet in Bavaria,

The following year, a colleague dies mysteriously while jogging in Stanley Park, Vancouver, sending Jake on another international quest, where he learns that his arch enemy from the previous year is still alive, working for a firm whose goal is to eliminate scientists who are trying to warn people about global warming. While at a funeral in Europe, he meets Sabrina, a gorgeous, very capable, mysterious lady who steals his heart. As they work together with law enforcement officials, they discover that a Serbian lady scientist is running an organization basically as a 'murder for hire' firm, supplying extremely deadly poisons she has concocted from 'natural' sources. After some of her employees and others involved die in a confrontation with police in Bregenz, Austria, Jake and his colleagues consider that the 'case is closed'.

Finally, after persistent coaxing from his friends and staff, Jake and Sabrina try to get away for some well deserved vacation 'down time'. As they have both travelled extensively in Europe, they decide to change scenarios, heading south for some sun and a different view, eventually choosing Argentina, and the beautiful, fascinating city of Buenos Aires. It sounded good when they planned the trip, but they did not realize a ghost from their past would follow them.

§

# Vengeance - Chapter - 1

Buenos Aires, Argentina

Jake Prescott stretched out his long frame on the soft pool lounge, enjoying the warmth of the Argentine sun, a pleasant contrast to the damp winter back in Vancouver. Although he could well afford these luxuries, he normally did not take advantage of them. This was a completely foreign experience for him, in more ways than one. After his staff had convinced him to take some time off, his girl-friend Sabrina added her voice to the crowd, and decided to join him in a little well deserved rest. She too was stretched out beside him, and Jake was thankful they had some privacy at their roof-top pool because of the many hungry glances that Sabrina attracted.

After the scary encounters they had experienced in Bregenz, Austria, the previous year, they both felt they deserved a break. Jake's nemesis, Kurt Landau had re-surfaced in Vancouver, killing one of Jake's colleagues, triggering another international search to find out who was behind the deaths of many of the world's top scientists, particularly those involved in the global warming research. Landau over extended himself, with a personal vendetta bent on destroying Jake and his associate, Jacques Manet of Interpol. Between the two of them, they had foiled Landau's plans the year before, plans to take over a huge international organization that could have meant billions to him.

Sabrina was relieved when she heard Landau was dead, as she herself had survived a serious encounter with Landau. Acting on an impulse one day, Landau had kidnapped Sabrina, locking her up in a secure location. Much to Landau's surprise, Sabrina was not the innocent young woman he thought she was, but a trained Swiss F.I.S. agent, who eventually tricked him, managed to take Landau's 9mm automatic and shot him three times in the chest. Subsequent followup rescue of Sabrina by the police discovered that Landau had been wearing a vest and had not been killed.

This time, Landau's vendetta went too far, and his 'employer', a Serbian woman behind many of these deaths, decided he had to be stopped. She sent her strong man lover to dispose of Landau, which resulted in a confrontation and shoot-out in a hospital in Bregenz, ending with both of them being killed.

Although they had all breathed a sigh of relief, nobody was fooled into thinking that was the end of their problems. The Serbian woman, Doctor Dejana Babić, a brilliant botanist/chemist who specialized in death potions, had gone to ground . . . not heard from in almost a year. They all referred to her as the 'Serbian Bitch', or the 'Damsel of Death', and they knew it was just a matter of time before she raised her ugly head.

Peter Wong, Jake's computer guru in Vancouver, was testing his IT skills, monitoring the internet and all forms of social media, searching for clues of her resumed activity. They knew her main consulting firm, the Sekhmet Group, was usually involved with clandestine influencing of her client's competition. This 'influence' took many forms, sometimes to the extreme of total elimination of the competition. Her extensive knowledge of biology and 'natural' poisons enabled her to produce some insidious methods of creating 'natural' deaths. Death by cardiac arrest, strokes, long term intestinal poisoning, and many others. This had resulted in the deaths of many scientists and environmental activists, some who were Jake Prescott's friends or colleagues. Peter was at a loss, he could not find any activity by the firm, or any mysterious deaths of their fellow scientists for the past year. After receiving another call, he welcomed the opportunity to call Jake direct.

"Peter! Good to hear from you." Jake answered. "This must be important, or you would not have called?"

"Yeah Jake . . . two things . . . first, an old friend and colleague of yours called . . ." Jake heard some paper rustling. "His name is Perez, Mateo Perez. I take it you know him?"

"Know him? Oh my God, I haven't heard from Matt in years. We took a few courses together at the Munich University, also got into a lot of trouble together. We were both in the same business." Jake stopped. "Is everything OK? What did he want?"

"Yeah, I think everything is OK, he just wanted to talk to you. I think some of the stories from last year finally trickled down, and he really wants to talk to you. I hope you don't mind, I told him you were already in Buenos Aires . . . boy, did that ever get him excited! Do you want his number?

"Yes please, just send it to my phone. I'll give him a call, it'll be good to catch up."

Jake paused, then added "You said you had a couple of things to discuss. What's the other one Pete?"

"Well, I'm a little concerned," he said to his boss, "about the Serbian Bitch. Alan and I have been watching her like a hawk . . . I don't know what she's up to. It's a little too quiet!"

"What do you mean?" asked Jake.

"Well Jake, you know what she's capable of. How skilled she is at keeping it under disguise. I'm afraid she's up to something that we don't know about!"

Jake nodded to himself as he reached again for some snacks and his glass of excellent Argentine Malbec. The old feeling came over him, the feeling he got when the 'big picture' was just out of sight. Jake's insight into problems like this was uncanny, and he too felt like Peter, something was going on and they were all missing it. "OK Peter, keep looking, I'll talk to Jacques . . . see if he's heard anything."

He was referring to Jacques Manet, his friend at Interpol. He had worked with Jacques on a couple of dangerous cases, cases that Jake had become accidentally involved in. Although Interpol agents do not normally work in the field, an unusual situation a couple of years ago threw the two of them together in an intense, life threatening situation which bonded them forever. Jacques Manet had become a good friend of Jake's, a friend that had saved his skin a couple of times, but always brought a smile to Jake's face when they met. Jacques' French father had supplied him with his name, but his London childhood and background was all English. A broad English accent . . . English manners and childhood mannerisms . . .stiff upper-lip and all that!

§

Suddenly Jake felt that his little vacation in the sun was over. Even the slightest mention of that Serbian doctor scared the hell out of him, as she was so skilled at what she did, you never knew how she might attack you. He remembered a lunch meeting he and Jacques Manet had near the Musée D'Orsay in Paris with a 'whistle-blower' contact who was trying to give them some important information. While they were enjoying a *cafe-au-lait* at a sidewalk bistro, the man was poisoned in front of their eyes, and they both missed catching the person who did it.

He glanced over to his left, at the most beautiful creature he had ever seen, Sabrina Wagner. Sabrina had been listening to his side of the conversation, guessing at the other side . . . a good guess, because she pretty well had it all figured out by the time Jake hung up.

# Vengeance - Chapter - 2

"Bloody Hell Jake! What are you doing in Buenos Aires?" Jacques' broad English accent boomed out of the speaker-phone Jake had set up between him and Sabrina.

"Don't you give me a bad time Jacques! You keep telling me I should take a vacation. That's just what Sabrina and I were trying to do."

"Well good for you old chap!" He chuckled. "And how is my favourite 'femme fatale', my lovely Sabrina?" Sabrina was definitely a favourite of Jacques, ever since she managed to disarm Kurt Landau and shoot him with his own gun. "Bravo for the Swiss!" he would shout.

"Hi Jacques!" answered Sabrina. I'm glad you don't mind us taking a little time off . . . or do you have something to tell us? Jake's staff back it Vancouver want to know if you've heard anything from the deadly Dr. Babić."

There was a long pause . . . too long for Jake's comfort. Jake jumped in again. "Jacques, what did you hear? What's going on . . . is she active again?"

"No, not that I've heard, that's the problem. As I mentioned to Peter and Alan in Vancouver . . . something is going on and we're not privy to it!" He stopped, then started as he remembered something. "Oh Jake, something else, this is why I was so surprised you were in Buenos Aires. I was talking to a fellow from our NCB in Buenos Aires yesterday, and the subject of your escapades with Dr. Babić came up. His name is Mateo Perez, apparently he knows you from the old days."

"Yes, Peter has already told me he was trying to get me in Vancouver. You say he's in your NCB here in Buenos Aires?"

"Yes, he's worked in the local police departments there for years and recently was transferred to the Interpol NCB."

"I'll call him right away, I'm sure we have a lot of catching up to do."

"Good! He really sounded quite urgent about it . . . I guess mainly to talk, but I think he's got some news about our Damsel of Death."

"Oh my God!" moaned Jake. "Here we go again! She's probably up to something down here, and we have no clue."

Sabrina moved a little closer to Jake, her flashing eyes and seductive lips distracting him while she said "Jake, you've been here before, think! You are good at figuring these things out."

"Yes, but only if I have some clues, some data to process."

"Then," she added "we'll get you some data, and this guy in Buenos Aires is a good place to start!" She stood up from her beach lounge, stretching her lithe body out, her skimpy bikini displaying all her attributes for Jake's benefit. "But right now, Mr. Prescott, we have a date back in our room, you said you needed another shower after all that Argentine sunshine." She gave Jake a look that he couldn't refuse. He had no choice but to follow her.

§

It was later that afternoon when Jake finally got around to phoning his friend and colleague Mateo Perez. After several minutes of surprise, emotional greetings and brief catching up, they agreed to meet at Jake's hotel for dinner that evening. Jake explained the hotel's location in the Recoleta district, which Mateo knew well.

When the couple entered the hotel lobby, they virtually took command of the room. Mateo was a tall, very muscular, dark eyed Argentinian, looking like he would be more comfortable riding a horse on the *pampas*. Elena was a perfect match, a tall, exotic beauty, who probably stayed fit doing the Tango with Mateo.

Once again, it was an emotional reunion as the two met in the hotel lobby. Jake introduced Mateo and his wife Elena to Sabrina. "So, Elena, you managed to hang on to this wild *Caballero*." Jake had met them both several years ago when they attended university in Munich. They made an interesting foursome as they started off to find a quiet table in the luxurious bar area.

"So, what is it Jake . . . four or five years?" Mateo asked.

"Don't I wish Matt, it been almost ten years. I don't know, but I'd guess one hell of a lot has happened since we both did this together." Jake grasped his cane tightly as they headed over to the corner table

Matt noticed Jake's cane. "I see you're still the useless cripple you were then." he laughed.

"Yeah, but I can probably still whip your ass in a tournament." Jake answered, remembering the Judo matches they used to have at university, where Jake had always managed to beat the heavier and stronger opponent. He looked again at Mateo's very fit, muscular frame, thinking maybe he would have some problems beating him now.

"Seriously, Jake, how is the leg? If I remember correctly, you were even on crutches for awhile when we were at university."

Jake shook his head as he too remembered those days. "Yes, I remember, Matt. It's O.K. now, as you can see, I graduated from the crutches to a walker, then to this cane. That leg just gives up when I least suspect it. The cane just gives me a little extra support when it decides to give out on me. Usually when I need it the most." he laughed. "And it's great for beating someone over the head if I can't use my judo. I think they have just taken my leg apart and put it back together too many times . . . maybe something is missing." Jake's leg and unreliable knee was alway a reminder of the loss of his parents years before in an accident that left him an orphan, with several years of pain and surgery.

So, for the next hour, they shared stories, caught up with each other's lives and made new bonds with the two ladies that accompanied them.

Matt finally changed the subject slightly by saying "Obviously I'm talking to the right man . . . and lady" he added, looking at Sabrina. "You guys have already been through this, so you have some idea of the long term effects, and seriousness of the situation."

"Situation? What situation Matt?" asked Jake quickly.

"Well first Jake, as Jacques most likely mentioned, I work here in the Interpol NCB, National Central Bureau." He paused again. "Remember when we had just finished our post grad work in Munich? We were going home to set the world on fire with our new-found environmental expertise! Well, it sounds like you did OK, but when I came home, nobody gave a damn about the environment, and especially nobody was willing hire anyone to do something about it. It's only been in recent years that that subject has gained any importance, especially since they started wiping out the Amazonian forests."

Jake nodded, knowing himself how the public awareness and priorities had changed over the years.

Mateo then added "So o o o, I had to get a job. Elena's uncle is a lawyer and he suggested the police force . . . the PFA, Policia Federal Argentina. They are the main, national policing organization throughout Argentina, and until recently, acted as a local law enforcement agency here in Buenos Aires. To cut this short, I managed to join, and I haven't looked back! I love the work and I'm good at it."

"But you said you worked for Interpol, at their NCB, here."

"Yes, that came a little later. All of these law enforcement organizations work very close together, or even in the same buildings. They even have some Special Forces Groups here, the guys that monitor terrorists, and that kind of activity. Then there is the Triple Border Group, monitoring the illegal activity in the Tri-Border region, near Puerto Iguazu, where they watch activity in Argentina, Brazil and Paraguay. They figure these activities amount to tens of billions of dollars."

"Wow!" exclaimed Jake . . . "Who knew?"

"I progressed in the organization . . . drugs, money laundering, human trafficking . . . and all the associated murder and mayhem." he finished with a wry smile.

"So what's going on now?"

"Two days ago, I was checking on a 'Red Notice' from Interpol head office. I think you know what that is?"

"Yes, they are bulletins of some kind alerting other offices about some bad guy . . . sort of an 'APB', as the TV programs call it."

"Yes, an 'All Points Bulletin' . . . be on the lookout for, etc."

Jake asked quickly "So what triggered your interest?"

"Let's go back a bit . . . you are aware of Interpol's use of facial recognition software?"

"Yeah, Jacques told me they were using it last year . . . it was good to keep track of Landau periodically."

"Right! Well, we've had some success with it here in Buenos Aires. Last year we arrested a internationally wanted murder suspect . . . a 33 year old Slovak wanted by Czech authorities listed in a Red Notice following a murder ten years ago . . . ten years ago! After Buenos Aires submitted images of the suspect and they came up with a match within 48 hours."

"Wow, that was fast!" exclaimed Jake.

"Well, that's not the end of it. Yesterday, there was another alarm . . . something did not look right. The software triggered an alert . . . but there was something to check. It indicated the suspect was already dead."

"Oh, that could be a problem."

"Well, yes and no. The interesting thing was he was killed during a case that you might be interested in, last summer in Bregenz, Austria!" Mateo ignored Jake's obvious desire for more information and continued. "I ended up calling Lyon . . . and talked with your Jacques Manet. He knew exactly who I was talking about."

"Oh my God!" shouted Jake, "Don't tell me Landau has come to life again!"

§

# Vengeance - Chapter - 3

They moved into the dining room for dinner, again taking a quiet corner table. Jake was slowly absorbing the last bit of information that Matt had revealed, but could hardly wait to hear the rest of the story. He could not believe how the evening was turning out. A happy reunion with an old school buddy was turning into a scary synopsis of a serial killer movie.

Jake could not wait. "Come on Matt . . . what are you saying . . . what did Jacques tell you . . . who are we talking about?"

"Well, to ease your pain, it was not Landau. He is truly dead this time. Jacques told me about Sabrina's run-in with him, and some of the other problems you had. This guy was the guy that killed Landau, then got himself killed. His name was Braco Dragonović."

"I don't understand, if he was killed . . . how was he triggered by your system a year later in Buenos Aires?"

"Well, that's another interesting part. It appears that Braco had an identical twin . . . Danko Dragonović! The software does not pick up the differences between identical twins."

Jake sat back to digest this information. Sabrina started to laugh. "OK, Mr. Smarty-pants! Is that enough information, enough data to start working on? I don't know about you, but I'm starving, and I suggest we put aside the doom and gloom stuff for awhile so we can get something to eat. After all, Jake, we're supposed to be down here on holidays!"

Everyone else agreed, so Jake had to back off. He grabbed one of the restaurant menus and said "O.K., gang, let's do this right! The Argentinians will choose the food, they know what's good, and I'll pay for it. Is that acceptable?"

"No, that won't do at all Jake, you two are visitors to our great city, so it's our treat. We are all going to have a special cut of Argentinian beef that's called an *asado*. You probably call it a barbecue. They serve a pretty good one here in this restaurant . . . not as good as out on Elena's *estancia,* but I'm sure you will enjoy it."

"Fine!" said Jake, "at least I can buy the wine! I've discovered this great Argentinian Malbec."

"Good choice, Jake." Matt answered.

'Shop-talk' eased off as they attacked their huge slabs of beef brought to their table. Their first taste of Argentinian a*sado* was a treat, and did not leave much room for conversation as they attempted to do the meal justice.

After the meal, they retired to a quiet section of the lounge, a spot where they could talk uninterrupted. The conversation picked up exactly where they left it.

"Well, later, when I called your office," Matt continued, "I wasn't even sure what I was talking about . . . but when I saw this guy's name, it began to make sense, and maybe my feelings and suspicions were valid." Matt paused in his discourse, almost like checking to see if his audience was prepared. "Have you heard of a company called 'X-Sells'?"

"No, I don't think so." Jake said slowly.

"Well, X-Sells Corp has been around for a few years, very successful at what they do, making tons of money doing it."

"What do they do, what do they make?"

"They don't make anything really . . . anything substantial. They sell an alternate version of the truth to the public . . . very efficiently I might add, a different truth, backed up by what they call 'scientific evidence'."

"I'm sorry," said Jake, I'm not quite understanding what you are saying. What do you mean 'an alternate version of the truth'?"

"Well, for example, 'Global warming is just an unproven myth', 'Cigarette smoking might even be good for you', 'Those seat-belt problems you had in your new car were not manufacturing faults, they were caused by you . . . not fastening it properly', and so on."

"That's crazy" shouted Jake across the table. "How can anyone say that in today's age, with all the evidence we have.?"

"Jake . . . it's done all the time! They twist the evidence, turn it around so that it seems like it proves their statements"

"So what's the result" asked Jake. "What does this all amount to, a bunch of nut-cases trying to dispute modern science?"

"No Jake, you've missed the point. These are not 'nut cases' . . . these are very well educated scientists, high priced lawyers, technical experts, and above all, some excellent sales people to put it all together in an effective package to sell to the public. They find little flaws in the data, or find a study that slants the data in a different direction, or just another way you can interpret the data. This company is making hundreds of millions of dollars a year peddling this crap!"

"Peddling it to who?" Jake asked.

"To any company who needs it, and can afford to pay for it. Just think . . .how many law-suits do you hear about every year, brought about by so-called faulty manufacturing, operator or pilot error, asbestos containing products, products not made 'child-proof'?" Matt continued, on a subject he had obviously researched in detail. "And . . ." he continued, "I almost hesitate to mention this one . . . it is becoming more and more obvious that many of the problems of global warming are not caused by the petroleum industry, but . . . would you believe it . . . the agriculture industry'?" He added "That last one by-the-way, is not going over too well in Argentina . . . So they are the firms I just mentioned that are hiring this crazy 'expertise' to back up their claims."

"Holeee Sh . . ." Jake exclaimed.

"The whole Argentine operation is run by a Franco Martinez, some Spanish speaking American 'super salesman'. When I say Spanish speaking, I don't mean Mexican or even Argentinian . . . I mean real Castellano, what you might call Castilian Spanish . . . I think he's from Madrid. He's really good! Not only that" continued Matt . . ." and here's the clincher . . .this X-Sells company is registered in Beograd, a wholly owned subsidiary of Sekhmet Consulting Group!"

"Oh my God!" both Jake and Sabrina gasped together. "That's what she's up to!" continued Jake.

"Who . . . what do you mean?" asked Matt. "What's going on?"

"I'm sure Jacques told you about our Serbian Bitch, the owner of the infamous Sekhmet Group?"

"Yeah, he mentioned how she had gone to ground . . . nothing active for almost a year." He suddenly reacted . . . realizing the connection. "*Madre de Dios*! Are you thinking she has come alive, just changed her stripes?"

"Could be . . . in fact, I'm sure of it!" Jake looked across to Sabrina, then back to Matt. "Correct me if I'm wrong, has this identical twin guy just flown in from Europe?"

"Yes, as a matter of fact, that was the next thing I was going to mention."

Jake started to rise. "We've got to talk to the guys back at the office, we should call Jacques."

Matt interrupted. "Don't bother, you guys . . . sit down and relax Jake . . . I'll deal with all that. After all . . . who's the cop here anyway? You guys are on vacation, remember?"

As they talked, Mateo remembered something. "Jacques had mentioned that the most frustrating thing about this woman's operation is that you can't get actionable evidence against her . . . something you can really pin on her."

"That's right," answered Jake, "We know she's behind a lot of this stuff, but we could never arrest her and take her to court."

"Well, be careful now. Just because she has a rep from one of her companies in Buenos Aires, doesn't mean she is doing anything illegal."

They talked well into the evening, both fascinated by what they were learning. The girls finally gave up and found a table of their own, where they could talk privately and quietly together. Elena's background mirrored Sabrina's in so many ways, only several thousand miles apart. Raised on a ranch or '*Estancia*' outside of Buenos Aires, Elena attended university, then studied law, eventually working at her uncle's law firm. She met Mateo when she took some extra courses in the university in Munich and the two have been inseparable ever since. Matt always drew upon her legal knowledge every time he decided to 'raise a little hell' as he put it, and Elena had enough fire to support Matt in any way she could.

Later, both Argentinians sat and listened in awe as Jake and Sabrina related the details of their adventures of the past couple of years and their exposure to the unexpected dangers of believing in global warming.

"That's insane!" Matt exclaimed as they paused in their stories. "How can anyone dispute the facts . . . the visual evidence all around us!"

"Well," commented Jake, "You just finished telling me about a firm that specializes in doing just that . . . turning those facts around to prove the opposite."

"Yes, but," He looked at Jake, suddenly appreciating the seriousness of what he was saying. "Oh my God, no wonder the world is going all to Hell! There are people who actually believe that crap!"

"'And they walk among us'," added Jake.

The girls had been listening to some of their conversations, and it was almost midnight when Sabrina interrupted the gloomy direction the subjects were heading. "Come on guys, lighten up! We should figure out what we're going to do tomorrow." she turned to Elena and Mateo. "It's the weekend, so I assume you guys have a couple of days off? O.K, you live here . . . what should we 'tourists' see first?"

Elena was delighted, adding "I'm sure we can keep you guys entertained . . . by the way . . . how long have you booked this hotel?"

Sabrina responded "We've only booked this week . . . we didn't know what else we'd be doing once we got down here."

"Good! I have some ideas for you . . . show you some 'real Argentina'".

# Vengeance - Chapter - 4

Elena stopped in front of their hotel late the next morning. "*Buenos Días* gang! A slight change of plans . . .we'll pick up Mateo at his work . . . he got called in early this morning, something important came up." she said as she pulled out into the Buenos Aires traffic. Jake had commented to Sabrina the day they arrived that he wouldn't want to deal with this traffic himself, so he was glad to have a local driver who was familiar with the city.

Sabrina complemented Elena on her driving skills. "My goodness! I'm sure glad you're driving, I couldn't deal with this."

"Oh, I'm sure you could, it's just a matter of what you're used to, and besides, this is just weekend traffic . . . you should see it on a week-day!" She laughed and added "And also, I know where we're going, that makes a difference."

"I'm sure it does" laughed Jake.

They were soon pulling up in front of a building, directly in front of a huge all black vehicle, more appropriately seen on a battlefield. "Wow" commented Jake. "What the Hell is that beast for?" he asked.

"Oh that thing! I think it's their pride and joy, it's a *Dongfeng Mengshi*, a kind of Warrior in Chinese. It's a Chinese Dongfeng Motor Group version of the Hummer . . . some sort of assault vehicle, probably bullet-proof . . . you notice, no windows?" She pointed to the other vehicle parked in front of the building. "These other blue vans are their usual city response vehicles, they are Italian built Iveco's."

Jake asked, "Why are they all marked with the Federal Police name and logo, same as on the building. I thought we were going to Interpol?"

"You don't miss much, do you Jake?" She laughed. "Matt still does a lot of work for the PFA, the *Policía Federal Argentina,* they work very closely with Interpol, so this is where he was needed this morning. At that point, her phone rang.

They watched her as she answered and talked to somebody, obviously Mateo. Her face grew serious as she nodded her head, her dark eyes growing wider. "O.K. Matt, I'll tell them."

"What was that Elena? Is something wrong?"

"Sorry guys, I'm afraid I'll be your tour guide for the day. Matt will be tied up for some time."

"What happened Elena . . . is everything O.K,?" asked Jake.

"They are still gathering information, but one of our big name politicians, a Tomas Romero, just dropped dead while making a speech at an environmental rally. They think it was a heart attack. He was a young man, but had lots of enemies, so somebody is asking questions, like 'was that really a heart attack?'"

"Oh My God" groaned Jake. "This sounds too familiar. What was the rally?"

"There's been a lot of opposition lately against the agriculture industry, especially the beef industry. Argentina is not the place to oppose the beef industry." she said, shaking her head. "You could make a lot of enemies very quickly."

"I can imagine." agreed Jake. "So what was this politician thinking?"

"Well, to fill in a little history, he's had a running battle with that firm X-Sells, they are telling everyone that beef is good for you, they grow it humanely, it's good for the environment, it fertilizes the ground, and all kinds of other 'facts' . . . and I have to say, a lot of them make sense."

"So . . . what?"

"Well, I'm sure you've heard all the opposition to eating meat . . . mainly the plant-based Vegan group. They are claiming that a lot of our climate problems are caused by the agriculture industry, mainly beef growing. My family has been growing beef on an *estancia* for several generations. All this talk has been hard on them, they are conscientious and are concerned with doing the right thing . . . but after-all, it's their livelihood."

Sabrina interrupted at this point. "In Europe, there has been a lot of activity with this controversy. Some of the universities have banned beef from their campuses as part of an effort to lower their carbon footprint." She stopped, holding up her hand to Jake, who looked like he had a question. "Which makes some sense, as a recent research paper published in the *Science* journal finds that beef produces 105 kg of greenhouse gases per 100 g of meat, and by comparison, tofu results in less than 3.5 kg."

"Wow, I'm sorry, I didn't know that." said Jake. "And here we've been blaming the petroleum industry for this."

"Not only that," continued Sabrina. "The World Health Organization has been stating for some time that hot dogs, bacon and other processed meats cause cancer. If nothing else, that fact alone should make you pause before you chomp down on a hot dog. Not only that, you'd think that governments would hesitate to subsidize industries that produce things that cause cancer."

"Are you saying we shouldn't have had that great *asado* last evening?"

They all laughed, remembering the wonderful time and delicious meal they enjoyed the night before. Jake continued "Back to the business at hand . . . Elena . . . what is Matt doing . . . can he join us later?"

"No, we'd better make our own plans. It sounds like he'll be tied up for some time." She looked again at Jake "You said 'this is all too familiar', or something like that. What did you mean Jake?"

"That's the M.O. of our Serbian bitch! People tend to drop dead of heart attacks, seizures, intestinal disorders, or any number of other ailments, brought on by a clever administration of one of her potions. This lady is a skilled scientist, she not only has years of botanical knowledge and experience, she's a very intelligent organic chemist. We've learned that some of her 'potions' are even more deadly than the natural version. We saw that in Vancouver last year, when my colleague was killed with her 'new and improved' version of Batrachotoxin. Just ask my lab guy, Alan Cook, he has all these things figured out, or at least partially figured out. . . she's always one step ahead of us."

He then asked Elena "Has Matt talked to Jacques at Interpol yet, or with Alan or Peter at my office?"

"I'm sure he's talked with Jacques, but I'm not sure what they've decided. And they are most likely checking out this new guy on the scene . . . especially since he's the brother of Dr. Babić's lover/strong man. He probably works for her as well. Don't worry Jake, it's all Interpol business now . . . I'm not always 'in the loop'".

§

Mateo Perez was indeed very busy with the death of Tomas Romero, the politician who stepped on somebody's toes. He had spent most of the morning gathering information from the local police who had been called to the scene. The scene being a political rally for one of the key proponents of Climate action, a relatively new group, advocating for less deforestation for agriculture. It was hard enough to convince Argentinians to cut back on cattle production, but by approaching the problem from a different direction Thomas Romero hoped to gain some support from his peers. The problem of deforestation was a major one in South America, especially in their neighbouring country, Brazil, where the burning of the Amazon forests to open up agricultural land had created world-wide concerns about both the pollution and the loss of carbon 'sinks'.

His discussion with Jacques Manet resulted in a serious plan of action, which Matt was implementing as fast as he could. Jacques agreed that the manner and circumstance of the man's death was a little too close to the M.O., or *modus operandi* he was very familiar with. When the Interpol facial recognition system picked up that guy at the Buenos Aires airport, it rang a lot of bells at headquarters. Jacques looked at the photos they sent him and compared them with the photos he had on file of the guy killed in Bregenz last summer. There was no doubt . . . they were the same guy . . . but further checks discovered he was Braco's twin brother! Jacques couldn't help but think to himself "How come the bad guys always come back to haunt you?" He knew instinctively that he must be the one that delivered Dr. Babić's 'package'. He recommended that Matt or the PFA medical people contact Alan Cook at Jake Prescott's lab in Vancouver. He might have some ideas to prove the point without waiting for a complete autopsy. The first thing he did was contact the field officers of the PFA, and advised them to collect any material they could that might be associated with the crime. Of course, they had already done that, but knowing what Jacques had told him, Matt offered a few more ideas to the investigating officers. Questions to ask: what, if anything did he eat, or drink? Who came close to him immediately prior to his collapse? Review all the video clips of the event, including the local news reporters' copies. If what he and Jacques suspect, they already had photos of their suspect, which they could compare against their local videos of the crowd at the rally. Next, obtain all of Thomas Romero's medical history for immediate review. Develop a list of all his competition, opposing views, rivals, people close to him, etc. The list went on and on, and Matt knew he would be tied up for the rest of the day, and probably a long time more.

He picked up his phone to call Elena.

## Vengeance - Chapter - 5

They returned to the hotel, none of them inclined to be a tourist for the remainder of the day. "Maybe we can do something tomorrow," said Jake, thinking that all he wanted to do was get on the phone to his office and to Jacques at Interpol.

"Come in Elena, we can at least have a drink and some lunch. I think we can write off Mateo for the day, he's going to have his hands full."

"I'm afraid you're right Jake, especially since this new twist has developed."

They headed immediately to the restaurant and once again, tried to pick a quiet area to sit. Jake was already on the phone, trying to reach his office. With the four hour difference in time, it was much easier to connect than what he was used to from Europe.

Shannon answered immediately. "Jake, what the hell is going on down there? Did you tell that bitch where you were going? How come she's surfaced in Buenos Aires . . ."

"Hold on Shannon, you've obviously been talking with somebody, you seem to know what's happening. First of all, I doubt very much if our 'Damsel of Death' is actually in Buenos Aires . . . which brings up the question "who is here?', who is working for that bitch?" He stopped, then added "I think we already know the answer to that question, but can you tell me what you've heard?"

Shannon slowed down, obviously concerned about her boss. They all loved Jake, but knew that he had a penchant for attracting trouble. Because of his innate ability to figure things out, see 'the big picture', he had foiled some of the plans of the wrong people, people who do not forget, people who hold grudges. Because of this skill, he was a perpetual target, someone that had to be eliminated.

The trouble from the previous year had culminated in a violent series of poisonings, shootings and even the kidnapping of Sabrina by one of the perpetrators. The deadly Dr. Dejana Babić was the main character involved, a specialist in deadly poisons. The problem was, nobody, not even Interpol could actually 'prove' any of these allegations in a court of law, so they were forced to stand by, waiting for her to make a move, a false move when they can get enough evidence to stop her. They even took her into custody once, and her lawyers had her released within the hour . . . no reasonable evidence to tie her to these events. After the climax in Bregenz the previous year, she had disappeared, 'gone to ground'. Not only Jake's IT crew, but Interpol and the FBI had been watching to see if she became active again. The clues they watched for were unexplained deaths or serious accident/injuries of leading scientists or activists in the environmental industry, especially on the subjects of global warming or other activities that might affect the profitability of a business.

The activity in Buenos Aires was the first indication that she had become active and was 'back in business'. The unexpected death of a middle aged man had the earmarks of her actions. Heart attacks can be brought on or simulated by several things, trace amounts of drugs that might or might not resemble the normal 'natural' chemicals in the body. The foxglove plant is well known to have deadly amounts of digitalis or digoxin, and is easily accessed by an expert plant chemist. Not only accessed, but fairly easily modified, manipulated or even enhanced by an expert chemist. Hydrangea blossoms, Oleander, and water hemlock are all familiar toxic plants. To a person who has years of plant studies, botany and organic chemistry training, modifying or rebuilding a portable poison to bring on a 'heart attack' is not a big challenge.

Other drugs can cause longer term deaths, convenient if you do not want the delivery of the poison to be connected with the result. A person might develop intestinal problems, nausea, kidney failure or a severe nervous condition, symptoms that might take hours or even days to show up. For instance, a small amount of Ricin, from the common Castor Bean, can cause severe vomiting, diarrhea, seizures over several days, many times resulting in death. It was used in 1978 to assassinate Georgi Markov, a journalist who spoke against the Bulgarian government. It had also been mailed to several U.S. politicians in other attempts.

Abrin, from the Rosary Pea, is very deadly, requiring only three micrograms to kill an adult. Jewelry makers have been made ill or died by pricking their fingers while working with the seeds, making prayer rosaries. The correct amount can cause organ failure within four days.

Shannon continued to explain to Jake. "We've been talking with Jacques, and with your man Mateo in Buenos Aires. He phoned to talk with Alan, getting some information on the poisons, how they might detect them, etc. They have a pretty good laboratory down there, so Alan was able to give them a few tips on how to proceed. If that was one of Dr. Babić's special doses, I'm sure they'll find out."

"Thanks Shannon, and what did Jacques say?"

"You'd better call him. He's glad they finally know where she is, or at least what she's up to, but is scared stiff that she might do something really crazy. I think he has a pretty good suspect in mind, that guy that looks like Landau's killer from last summer. He thinks he was his brother."

"Yes, Jacques mentioned him, and explained to Matt."

"He'll probably tell you more, but we all want you to be extra careful Jake, you know how much that woman wants to get even with you."

"Thanks Shannon, I'll call him right after lunch. As I said before, the question remains . . . I doubt she is in Buenos Aires personally, so besides this other guy, could there be somebody else involved?"

§

Doctor Dejana Babić was glad she had shut down her network before the incident in Bregenz came to a climax. From what she learned since then, both Interpol and Jake Prescott's gang were stymied, confused, and wondering when she would resurface. So she waited . . . she was in no hurry . . . she had learned long ago that patience can be an effective weapon. Not only does it provide extra time to plan, it also confuses your enemy, makes them unsure of what to do next. Dejana had always been an ardent fan of Sun Tzu's "The Art of War, where he writes "The *whole secret lies in confusing the enemy, so that he cannot fathom our real intent."*

After about six months of her 'hibernation', in addition to sending her 'lover' on an assignment, she reactivated one of her companies, one which had not been active for some time, one which Interpol and Prescott knew nothing about. It was a very profitable venture, and only required someone on site to monitor the results and report to her. The company, X-Sells, was a high tech science-based firm staffed with high paid scientists and salesmen that could convince anyone of anything. They normally operated legitimately as an environmental consultant, but occasionally she asked them to do an extra 'selling' job.

She had learned years ago that most people only hear what they wanted to hear. If you are a smoker, you did not want to hear that it was bad for you, you wanted to hear that the jury was still out, that maybe it's not so bad for you after all. For this information, tobacco companies would pay huge sums of money to convince the public that smoking is OK. The same thing held true on many fronts, and more recently they were convincing many companies that the global warming scare was just that, a scare, which had no real basis in the truth. Even with the huge amount of scientific evidence to the contrary, they managed to dig out other research, 'studies' done by obscure companies or think-tanks that indicated that perhaps things were not as bad as originally thought. Every bit of doubt they could cast on the popular beliefs, added to their profit line.

Her first 'test run' was in Argentina, a fast growing economy that depended heavily on agriculture. They were also faced with the growth of opposition to cattle farming, the destruction of forests to plant crops to raise cattle. The inefficiencies of cattle farming, and the large greenhouse gas 'footprint', were the main targets of the activists and 'tree huggers'. Activists and 'tree huggers' that might have to be eliminated.

# Vengeance - Chapter - 6

Danko Dragonović smiled to himself, very pleased with the results. Dejana's little gift had been delivered and had produced the desired result. As a temporary and anonymous waiter in the catering firm working on the rally, it was easy for him to drop his little package into the politician's drink, his favourite *Yerba Mate*.

He was thinking back, remembering how he felt when he learned his brother had died. Not only his brother, but his twin brother! Braco had died heroically in Bregenz after killing that idiot Kurt Landau. They had to depend on their contact in Interpol to copy certain emails for their information, but they were both satisfied that they had a true account of what happened. Dejana had sent Braco to stop Landau . . . stop his out of control need for revenge, his personal vendetta against Jake Prescott. The assignment ended in a gun battle between the two men in the hospital where they were holding Landau, and Braco's final dramatic sacrifice of taking a capsule of Dejana's special poison. The entire episode affected both Dejana and himself and resulted in a three day mourning session and sex orgy, fuelled by *Rakija,* Serbian Raki spiked with Dejana's exquisite aphrodisiac potion. Dejana had always enjoyed these sessions with her two 'boy-toys', the Dragonović twins, but realized she would now have to be satisfied with one of the twins. She always suspected that Danko would be up to the challenge, and the past few days had proven that point. They were both drained, both mentally and physically.

Danko felt excited to finally get back in the field and actually do something. For the past year, he had watched his brother come and go, working on exciting projects, travelling around the world. Even though his brother's last assignment had resulted in his death, Danko still felt he had missed out on so much, and was anxious to get out and prove himself, both for his own satisfaction and the anticipated rewards he would receive from Dejana.

The assignment to Buenos Aires had confirmed his feelings. For the past few weeks, he had enjoyed everything this amazing city had to offer, the warmer weather, the food, the wine, and the beautiful women. His part time job as a waiter for the catering firm had placed him in a perfect position to complete his first 'delivery'. He realized he could not work there for long, so he quickly moved back to his usual job as a bouncer at *'La Bebida Fuerte'*, or 'strong drink' bar and restaurant. This bar was also a well known *Milonga* or tango hall in the San Telmo district of Buenos Aires. Although Danko did not have the *Spetsnaz* training like his brother, he did have a working knowledge of Spanish, and his background and years of experience sparing with his brother made him a natural fit for a physical job like a bouncer or enforcer. Again, the job did not pay much, but the bar had an excellent reputation, which gave him access to many important people, politicians and visiting international dignitaries.

Although Danko felt good about himself and his accomplishments so far, he had no idea that the Interpol facial recognition system had flagged his entrance into Argentina a few weeks ago as he arrived at the airport. Even if he had known this, he would not have worried as he did not have a record, was not wanted in any country, and did not even class his latest project as being a problem, as he felt there was no way he could be blamed for a politician's heart attack. So Danko made no adjustments to his routine. He was lucky to get the temporary job with the catering firm. He was sure they did not know where he lived or what his real name was, nor could they connect him in any way to the event at the political rally.

So he was surprised to see an urgent message arrive on his phone the next day. A message from Dejana. Although he wasn't worried, Dejana was! The message basically told him to get out of town, return home asap. "Screw that!" he exclaimed to his phone . . . "I'm just starting to have fun."

With that, he stuck the phone in his pocket and headed out for some lunch.

§

Dejana was definitely worried . . . and a little confused. She had just heard that Interpol had tracked Danko to Buenos Aires, and suspected him in the death of Tomas Romero, the politician who had just died in front of a crowd at an environmental rally. "How did they know?" She asked herself. "How did they catch on so fast?" When she did not receive any confirmation from Danko, she also started to get angry. She knew what appetites Danko had, appetites she herself had helped feed. She was worried now that a person like that, turned loose in a hotbed of beautiful women, sexy Tangos, wine and booze, was going to be difficult to control. She returned to her 'office' to contemplate her next move.

§

Jake Prescott and Sabrina Wagner were also contemplating their next move. After discussing the situation with Jacques at Interpol, and his staff in Vancouver, they decided it was up to Mateo and his people to track down the person they suspected of the crime, someone who had entered Argentina a few weeks ago and had basically disappeared. The P.F.A. had reviewed the videos of the rally and everything associated with it. They were pretty sure the poison had been delivered by one of the waiters, but there was no proof, no facial recognition to confirm this. Even after reviewing the videos, the other personnel on site and the catering firm were not sure which one of their employees it was. The firm hired some of their help anonymously and only for short terms, individual events.

Interpol's 'Red Notice' had been reactivated, this time with a different name. From what Jacques Manet's experts had determined, Braco's twin brother was Danko Dragonović. Further tracking from earlier in the month discovered how he had arrived at Buenos Aries. They back-tracked further through several airlines and routes to find out when and where he started. Danko's odyssey had begun at the Nikola Tesla airport in *Beograd*. Jacques had suspected the Belgrade connection, but it was comforting to discover exactly when and where he started.

After passing all this information on to his colleagues in Argentina, he quickly punched out Jake Prescott's number on his phone. A message greeted him to call back later. "Damn!" he exclaimed. "Just when you want him, he's loafing in the sun down in Argentina!" He pressed his intercom button and said "Annette, could you please keep trying to get Jake Prescott on the phone for me?" He then called again, this time to Jake's office in Vancouver.

"Shannon . . . its Jacques Manet in Lyon."

"Oh Jacques, I'm so glad you called. I suppose you've heard about Jake and Sabrina down in Argentina . . . they figure that the Serbian Bitch is in operation down there."

"Yes Shannon, we've been trying to keep tabs on her for over a year now." He paused, then added "But I don't think it is her, we think it is the brother of the guy who killed Landau . . . I think he was sent to avenge his brother's death."

"Oh my God! Things are getting complicated again Jacques. I'm afraid for Jake, he's likely to get himself deeply involved in this . . . and he's supposed to be down there on vacation with Sabrina!"

"Don't worry Shannon, he's in good hands . . . Sabrina is with him." He laughed as he tried to sound confident for Shannon. Jacques remembered just how deadly Sabrina could be in a pinch, but in reality, he was just as worried as Shannon, and decided to check again with the Buenos Aires N.C.B..

# Vengeance - Chapter - 7

Malina Aleksov left Jacques Manet's office feeling a little better. She had been working for Interpol for almost two years now as a translator, and during that time, she had been passing confidential information back to Dejana Babić in Beograd. She had started this when Dejana, a distant relative, had made her an offer she could not refuse. It was a generous offer combined with a serious threat to her family. During the operation the previous year in Bregenz, Jacques had discovered what she was doing, and basically gave her a choice. Either lose her job and get arrested, or work for Jacques as a double agent to keep up with Dejana's actions. Jacques always liked Malina, and she was a very capable translator for both Serbian and French, and helped out with other Slav languages as well. Her job gave her the perfect opportunity to monitor Dejana's activity, and also the ability to pass on false or misleading information from the Interpol operation. Of course, Malina accepted Jacques' offer, and they had worked together ever since. Things had been very quiet for almost a year, but recently had heated up. To Malina's surprise, Dejana had contacted her about a month previous, asking her to monitor the activity in the Argentina N.C.B., or emails from Jacques to anyone else. She complied, keeping Jacques aware of each move. She also knew that if Dejana ever discovered her 'treason', her life would be in danger, as

Dejana did not tolerate anyone working against her, or even trying to quit her secret network of 'agents'. She recalled from the previous year the contact person Dejana used in Paris had tried to quit, but made the mistake of contacting Interpol to confess some of his actions. This promptly resulted in his death while having coffee with Jacques and Jake Prescott at a Paris sidewalk Bistro. A death still not resolved completely or legally determined who the perpetrator was. That was Malina's biggest fear . . . she knew how efficient Dejana's network was and how deadly her poisons were.

Her meeting with Jacques Manet had provided her with some additional information to pass on to Dejana. Jacques had asked her specifically to mention this to Dejana, but also to try to make it sound like it was secret that nobody should know, and she was lucky to learn this information to pass it on. Malina smiled, she could do this, she knew exactly how to develop a message to pique Dr. Babić's interest and cement her relationship with her. Malina always felt she was walking a tight-rope to keep Dejana supplied with intelligence she felt was useful, and satisfy her immediate employer Interpol. Of course Jacques helped her by supplying almost everything she passed on, information that was current and fairly valuable, but not damaging to their work. This time it was an experiment, something they were going to try to catch their elusive 'Damsel of Death'. The only thing that worried him was that Jake Prescott was the 'bait' in their trap.

§

Luckily, Jake received all of the urgent messages at once and decided to call Jacques. "What's up Jacques? It seems I just talked to you, has something else happened?"

"Not really Jake. You might not like what I'm about to tell you. Is Sabrina listening?"

"Yes, go ahead Jacques, what's happening?" Sabrina answered.

"I going to try a little experiment. I realize I should have checked with you first, but my timing was off." He paused, not sure how he was going to say this. "We're going to set a trap Jake, for our lady in Beograd. Unfortunately, you are the bait."

"What . . . what are you saying Jacques?" asked Sabrina quickly over the phone. "What crazy scheme have you guys come up with."

"Well, it's not that crazy my dear, we've just leaked the information to Beograd that Jake is currently in Buenos Aires on vacation. I wanted to get that bit of information to her while she still had her man Danko on site."

"Jeez, thanks, you crazy bugger. What am I supposed to do if this guy decides to dispose of me, I don't even know him, probably couldn't recognize him if I bumped into him on the street."

"That's OK Jake, calm down. He doesn't know you either. Mateo can give you some photos of him, at least you should be a little prepared."

"Things are different here Jacques. I'm not playing on a level playing field. I'm not used to the country, the language, or the rules." He suddenly remembered something. "And I don't have my Sig Sauer 9mm to back me up!", referring to a handgun he had acquired a couple of years previous that had saved his skin more than once.

"I understand Jake, but you'll just have to rely on your friend Mateo. He's an Argentinian, from Buenos Aires, works for Interpol and the PFA, speaks the language, and is probably heavily armed. What more do you want?" he laughed.

Jake looked at Sabrina, who was actually taking this news much better than Jake was. She was actually laughing. Jake looked at her, baffled. "And what the Hell is so funny young lady?" he asked.

"And to think," she said, still laughing, "I could still be plugging away at my part-time job in the tourist office in Bregenz, perfectly safe!"

"And probably bored to tears." commented Jake.

She added "In any case, I'll have my little 'Baretta 'Pico' . . . I'l have to talk to Mateo, to see if I can get permission to carry it here."

Jake was surprised. "You brought your .38? How did you get it on the plane?

"Jake, you keep forgetting I am a law enforcement officer, I'm allowed certain freedoms, but It was checked in baggage anyway."

Jake got serious and added "I'm sorry Sabrina, I hadn't anticipated we'd be the bait in a deadly trap when we planned this little holiday."

"I understand Jake," she said, "It just struck me as funny, how my life has changed since I met you."

"Well, I think we're going to have to plan, some contingency plan to keep safe. We don't want this guy sneaking up on us." He stopped, his mind in a turmoil. "Can you call Elena . . . find out if Mateo is available for dinner tonight. I think we have to have a war-plan."

§

Danko was a little surprised when Dejana phoned again . . . this time a voice call, not a text message. "Hello?" He answered, tentatively.

"Jesus Danko! Why aren't you answering my texts?"

"Because I didn't like what you were asking." he said, with a little more force than usual. "I'm having a little fun down here and I don't really want to go back to Beograd . . .not now."

Dejana's eyebrows went up, thinking that she would have to be careful handling this man, he obviously had a mind of his own, and might not be as easily handled as she thought. Thinking quickly, she added "That's O.K. Danko, I was just a little concerned. There are a couple of things I had to tell you."

"Like what?" he asked, realizing she was serious.

"Well, first, Interpol knows you are in Buenos Aires, they caught you with facial recognition when you arrived a couple of weeks ago."

"But how . . . I've never had a record or been arrested?"

"I think the system thought it was your brother . . . and rang some bells."

"Oh Jesus! Ghosts from the past, and what is the other thing you wanted to tell me?"

"Oh, you'll love this one!" Dejana said, a seductive undertone to her voice, "Jake Prescott and his girl friend are both in Buenos Aires."

"Wha . . . here?"

"Yes my dear, and I think we have to discuss what our next move is, what surprise we might dream up for our friend!"

Danko couldn't believe what she was saying. Although he didn't have the vendetta against this Prescott fellow that Dejana had, he felt obligated to listen and participate as much as he could . . . both in memory of his brother, but also for the love and passion he felt for Dejana.

# Vengeance - Chapter - 8

Dejana Babić was glad she had told Danko about Prescott's location. She leaned back in her lounge facing the fireplace. She could feel its heat over the outside of her body, as the Raki warmed her inside. She only wished that Danko was here to warm up her other desires.

As she thought about Danko and their current problem, she knew between the two of them, they should be able to come up with a plan for this thorn in her side. But she was confused, how did that Prescott guy catch wind of her plans? Apparently, from the reports from her 'agents', Prescott had been in Buenos Aires for over a week, supposedly taking a vacation with his girlfriend Sabrina Wagner. Dejana didn't believe it for a minute, of all places in the world, why Buenos Aires? Just after Danko arrived on his 'assignment'? Something didn't ring true, it was too much of a coincidence, and she didn't believe in coincidences.

§

Matt was exhausted. Coordinating all of the checks and double checks related to the event had dragged him down. Not so much by the activity, because he was lucky enough to have a lot of extra manpower supplied by the Argentine police force. What was definitely exhausting and disappointing was the lack of actionable results. Hours of pouring over videos of the event, zooming in on faces, confirming identities of every person in the video, every one except the guy who dropped the poison into his *Mate* cup. He couldn't believe it . . . nobody knew who this guy was . . . even though they were positive that someone in the catering group had served the man the *Mate* that had poisoned him. They were pretty sure that one of the videos showed how he did it, but his face and any distinguishing features were not clear, as all the waiters wore the same uniform and all looked alike, unless seen face-on. Rapid analysis of what was left in his cup confirmed their suspicions. As he read the report, he looked twice into his own *Mate*, then smiled as he sucked on it again, hoping the caffeine would give him a boost. His lab people had called Jake Prescott's chemist, Alan Cook in Vancouver to discuss technique. His chemists were amazed at the detail they received from Vancouver. Apparently, Alan had done his homework on the subject, ever since their experiences from the year before, learning that many variations of medicines can be derived from the common foxglove plant. Many of these 'medicines' can be very poisonous if not handled or dispensed in the correct way. Alan initially showed them some quick short-cuts to determine what poison they were dealing with, specifically what plant was the guilty party, as there were several that could bring on cardiac problems. Once that was determined, they proceeded to a more specific analysis.

The most significant compound derived from the common foxglove is digitalis, or its deadlier versions of digitoxin, digoxin and other cardiac glycosides. A few shortcuts in their analysis procedures helped to shorten their work, and they narrowed it down very quickly to what they suspected. A very strong glycoside variation that did not require much to bring on an acute cardiac arrest. But who, he asked himself?

Matt remembered some of the stories he heard from Jake and Sabrina the evening before. This 'Serbian Bitch', as they called her, was an expert in this field, an expert in modifying natural poisons, plant or animal, to fit her needs, change the response time, the reaction time, the physical symptoms, the severity of the reactions.

By the time he and his lab people had worked on the problem for just the first day, they had a pretty good idea of what had happened. Considering what they had learned from Interpol Headquarters and Jake Prescott, the question of 'who' became obvious, but they were still in the dark as to what her motive was, who would order such a fatal move, and eventually, who was it that dispensed the dose? He began to understand the frustration of the others, when he realized there was nothing positive, nothing actionable that could definitely connect this man's death with this crazy bitch in Serbia. Matt then decided he had enough information to share with Jacques Manet at Interpol and with his friend Jake. It was later that evening when he finally got a chance to talk to Jake on these points.

§

Danko was pissed off. How in hell had Interpol triggered him as soon as he entered the country? Of course he already knew the answer to that question. The actions of his brother last year had set up an alert in Interpol records, a file that was still active. When the stupid damned machines looked at his picture, it rang the bells, much to the surprise of those monitoring the output. Nobody had taken the trouble of telling the damn machine that he was dead . . . or at least the face in the file was dead.

As he thought about the problem, and especially Dejana's reaction to the problem, he knew he had to do something about it. He had nothing against this Jake Prescott, or his girlfriend, but he knew somehow he wasn't going to have any fun in Buenos Aires until he disposed of this glitch.

He had enough smarts to know he didn't have to do this personally, he would be clever like Dejana and have somebody else do it. His work at *La Bebida Fuerte* had put him in touch with all kinds of interesting contacts since he had arrived. Places to buy booze, drugs, women, and any other kind of entertainment. He made a point to ask around for other services he might require . . . services that aren't normally advertised.

§

Matt finally closed up his computer and prepared to go home. He called Elena, and was glad to learn that she had made arrangements for dinner again with Jake and Sabrina. As he closed the drawer on his desk and was starting to lock it, he stopped, pulled out his holstered service pistol, then closed and locked the drawer. Normally, he did not take his pistol home, but with the activity and heightened alerts he experienced today, he just felt a little more secure with his trusty Bersa Thunder 9 strapped under his arm. Most of the PFA officers carried a standard Glock 17, a favourite of law enforcement around the world, but Matt preferred the Argentine manufactured Bersa, this 'Thunder 9' model specifically. He felt much better as he closed his office and left the building

As his taxi approached Jake's hotel, Matt found himself looking around more than usual, feeling a little foolish as he saw nothing out of place, nothing that was a threat. He hitched the holster up a little under his arm as he left the taxi and walked into the hotel.

# Vengeance - Chapter - 9

Danko's meeting with his 'contractor' was very discreet, but in some ways quite amusing. Danko had seen enough Hollywood movies to categorize this meeting as a low budget movie scenario. First there was an identity procedure, making sure he wasn't some kind of cop. Then there was the location to decide on, somewhere that they both knew, yet would not be recognized. For Danko, that was easy enough, he wasn't really known almost anywhere in Buenos Aires. And then, of course, Danko wanted to make sure that whoever he dealt with would be willing and capable of doing what he wanted. Then there was the price to agree upon. Danko had some money he had brought from Europe, and he knew he had access to more, but he was reluctant to commit himself too much to an unknown character.

So he managed to keep a straight face during the negotiations, and they finally agreed on a price for several stages of action, depending on what might be required. The first stage was to approach Jake Prescott and his girlfriend and 'convince' them they should leave Buenos Aires . . . they were in danger . . . something to make their life . . . make their vacation uncomfortable.

The next step, Danko was almost embarrassed to admit, he had no idea where Prescott and his girlfriend were staying, which hotel? So he had no choice but to put the project on hold until he could learn and pass on this information.

§

As soon as Mateo walked into the hotel, Elena spotted him from across the huge entrance lobby. She walked quickly across, speaking over her shoulder at Jake and Sabrina. "Here he is, better late than never!" she said. "Oh Matt, I'm so glad you could come. Who knows how long these two can visit, so we have to take advantage of the time we have."

Jake rose to meet Matt, a look of concern on his face. He knew what Matt had been involved with all day and was almost afraid to ask. "Well Matt, were we correct? Was it some delightful dose that your politician sipped with his Mate?"

"You're right Jake, your guy in Vancouver was a big help to speed up the process. They narrowed it down very quickly to some derivative of digitalis, but I left it at that point. I'll let the chemists do their thing! There still remains, however, as they keep reminding me from Head Office, we still don't have a solid connection to your gal in Beograd."

"I didn't figure you would, she's much too clever to leave any clues pointing to her." He stopped a moment, then added "other than she's the only person we know that is that good at making these potions!"

They moved over to a table at the far side of the lounge, a little more private than the entrance lobby. The girls were instantly involved in discussions about what they were going to see tomorrow. Jake couldn't help noticing the slight bulge in Matt's jacket as they sat down to enjoy their drinks.

"So what's with the gun, Matt?" He commented. "You weren't packing one the first evening we met. Has something changed?"

"Oh, I didn't think you'd notice," responded Matt with a bit of a laugh, "After a day like today, I just slipped it on when I left the office . . . made me feel a little better."

"I know what you mean," said Jake, "Now I feel a little naked without my Sig."

"Nothing to worry about Jake, just my paranoia after too many years in the business. We're just going to enjoy the evening and the girls can plan out what we're up to tomorrow."

They carried on with their visit and another excellent meal, but Jake kept wondering if Matt was telling him everything, if everything was OK. His experiences during the past years cautioned him to be alert, and his sixth sense told him that all was not well . . . something was brewing.

§

Jacques Manet and Malina Aleksov were meeting in his office. "I'm worried Malina, worried that Dejana is going to discover our little deception, and take some serious action against you. Are you sure she does not suspect anything?"

Malina was also worried. She had been worried ever since the two of them had started this clandestine escapade. "Jacques, I don't think so, I certainly hope she doesn't." Malina was more than worried, she was constantly thinking about Dejana . . . about what she might do if she suspected Malina's duplicity. She was not only worried, but from time to time thought about a way to get away from the problem to eliminate the threat if the chance ever presented itself.

"Well I hope not, nothing has changed in her actions, or reactions." He checked a file on his computer screen and added "She hasn't had much going between her and Danko for a couple of days, because he basically cut her off. But something must have changed, because today Danko asked if she knew where Prescott was staying . . . which hotel?"

"I know" Malina said, "She asked me that. I didn't know the answer, or if I should tell her."

"OK, I just learned that myself. Jake contacted me in case I couldn't get him on his phone. He's still getting used to his smart phone and he doesn't trust it."

Malina looked a little confused as she was young enough that she had never met anybody not comfortable with a smart phone.

"Never mind Malina, that's a private joke." Jacques commented to ease her concern. "In the meantime, maybe the next time you communicate with Dejana, you can mention that Prescott is staying at the Etoile Hotel in the Recoleta district."

"Thank you Jacques, but, how would I find that out? I have to have a logical reason of how I came to know this."

"Of course!" Jacques said, "You can say you saw it on an email from Jake . . . that should explain it."

"Good, thanks, one thing more, I want to take some vacation soon to visit my family in Beograd. I'm afraid I might run into Dejana . . . by accident. What would I say?"

"Oh!" Jacques was surprised at this. He didn't think Malina had much to do with her family still. But then he remembered that Dejana had used threats against Malina's family to coerce her to spy for her. "Well Malina, just act normally, act as if nothing had changed . . . can you do that?"

"I think so, I just have to remember that I am working for the 'good guys'," she said, "I'm not the one going around poisoning people."

"Well," said Jacques, "You're going to have to be careful not to say something like that. You are not supposed to know all that." Jacques thought a moment, then added "Actually, a little vacation trip home might be good . . . it would be something she wouldn't expect you to do if you were fearing for your safety. It might even be a good idea to let her know what you plan.

How well did you know her? Did you ever get together socially before?"

"Well not really. I met her a few times, she was close to my aunt and uncle."

"O.K., you'll just have to be careful, play it by ear. In the meantime, I'll check . . . maybe we could help finance the trip . . . at least help you with the costs. Which brings up what happened last year, when you were supposed to poison me. Did you ever resolve that difference . . . does she know why you didn't go through with it?"

"Yes, I forget now what I said, but she was satisfied with my excuse. I think that was when Mr. Landau was involved . . . she had other things to think about."

"Good, then we're good to go!" Jacques watched her leave his office, then asked his secretary to get Jake on the phone, he had to tell him that his stalker now knew where he was staying.

# Vengeance - Chapter - 10

As soon as Danko received the email about Prescott's location, he grabbed a cab and headed over to the Recoleta District to check it out. Recoleta was an upscale residential area in downtown Buenos Aires, known for its beautiful old architecture and the famous Recoleta cemetery. One of the biggest attractions in the cemetery was the tomb of Eva Peron, the beloved 'Evita', as she is known to Argentinians. Her tomb and many other monuments for famous people made the Recoleta Cemetery a huge tourist attraction in Buenos Aires. The Etoile Hotel was a moderate high-end hotel on the edge of a park right next to the cemetery, and Danko decided to leave the cab and walk around a bit, become familiar with the neighbourhood, one quite different to where he was staying. After he had soaked up enough of the ambience, he returned to his own hotel and made a call to his newly hired 'contractors' to advise them where Prescott was staying. He then headed off to San Telmo for his 'work', at *La Bebida Fuerte*. He tried not to think too much about Mr. Prescott's fate, as it could take a day or several days before his 'contractors' have a chance to deliver the message.

§

At the same time, his 'contractors' were stymied. They knew their target's name, and where he was staying, but they had no idea what he looked like, and how they were going to separate him from the rest of the guests so they could deliver their message. Luckily, one of the gang, Pedro Vasquez, had enough smarts and experience to know how to do this. He arrived near the hotel close to dinner time, and parked some distance away. Then he waited until many of the guests had come down to the dining room for their evening meal. As it happened, Jake and his friends had just gathered and were in the lounge enjoying their drinks. Pedro entered the hotel and headed over to the bar and ordered a drink. He looked around, spotting several groups enjoying the evening, not sure if any of them contained his objective. Pulling out his phone, he called the hotel front desk, to page a Mr. Prescott, to come to the desk for an important telephone call.

He watched as the message came over the PA system. Before long, a tall man with a cane rose from the lounge area and walked over to the desk. There appeared to be some confusion as the message was delivered, but nobody was on the phone. The man finally returned to his group of friends. Pedro watched closely remembering details of the man, tall, with a cane. "This might be easier that I thought" went through his mind.

He left the hotel and as soon as he was outside, he called the hotel again. He feigned confusion, saying he had tried Mr. Prescott's room earlier, and he wasn't there. Could you please confirm his room number? The hotel, like most hotels, was reluctant to give out that information, but Pedro had enough experience at this game that before long, with a combination of confusion and bold statements, he finally knew exactly which room this Prescott was registered in.

Pedro returned to this car, changed his jacket and pulled a matching baseball cap down over his head. Picking up a small briefcase, he reentered the hotel and immediately went to the elevator. Within minutes he was on Prescott's floor and in front of his door. Knowing that Prescott would be occupied with friends for dinner for some time, he quickly picked the lock and let himself in.

Normally, when he pulled this little exercise, it was to burgle the place and steal something specific. He looked around, and seeing nothing of great value, decided to stick to his main objective . . . scare his prey and his girl-friend.

§

When Jake and Sabrina returned to the room later that evening, they couldn't believe what they saw. Everything they owned was dumped on the floor, their suitcases emptied, personal items scattered around, papers strewn around, and their clothes thrown about. Jake immediately went to the phone to call hotel security. That's when he noticed the blinking message signal on the room phone. Before he rang the hotel desk, he listened to the message. A low, grumbly voice came through very clear. *"¡Sal de la cuidad, vete a casa, muy pronto!"*.

Jake looked over at Sabrina, both a little confused and frightened with this turn of events. Jake's command of Spanish wasn't great, but good enough to understand the message. *"Get out of town, go home, right away!"* Sabrina was already on her phone, not to security, but to Elena.

"Elena, thank God you're there! Tell Matt that we've been broken into at the hotel and he should come right away. No police . . . just Matt. There is a message he should hear."

Sabrina listened for a moment, then said "No, we haven't called hotel security yet . . . I thought you and Mattt should see this first. Who knows how this is linked . . . or if it is."

Jake was thankful that Sabrina was with him, her training and experience valuable in situations like this. She reacted very cool and in control, and seemed to know exactly what to do next.

He would have called the hotel front desk, but after hearing Sabrina's call to Elena, he realized it might be the best move, especially considering the other things going on in their lives. He couldn't help but think to himself "Jesus! Is it always going to be this difficult to get a decent vacation?"

§

It didn't take long for Matt and Elena to arrive, as they hadn't even returned home yet. Both had concerned looks on their faces. The first thing Matt did was to listen to the telephone message. "Yes, you pretty-well have it Jake, someone is telling you to get out of town and go home, *muy pronto!* right away!"

"But that doesn't make any sense Matt. Who the hell would want me to go home, what am I doing, what threat am I to anyone?"

"I don't know Jake, but somebody is getting nervous . . . maybe someone who is familiar with your reputation . . . or maybe just someone who knows you are here and is becoming uncomfortable with you being here . . .with you snooping around!"

Sabrina added "Yes, and the only person I can think of that might feel that way is a long ways from here, hiding in her lair in Serbia!"

They all stopped short, looking at each other, suddenly realizing what Sabrina was saying. Jake was shaking his head. "Yes, I see what you are saying Sabrina, but what does she hope to achieve by warning us to go home? What does she think that I am doing here, and what does she think this little exercise is going to accomplish?"

"I don't know Jake," said Matt, "but she's sure got our attention!"

# Vengeance - Chapter - 11

The rest of the evening was very busy and tiring. Matt went down to the front desk and introduced himself, advising them why he was there. He also told them he did not want hotel security or many of the staff knowing what had happened, as he would rather keep the event quiet. The hotel was glad to oblige, as they did not want the story to get out to other guests. They arranged for Jake and Sabrina to move into the room next door. Matt wanted his crew to go over the room before anyone else could contaminate the scene. Jake and Sabrina carried some of their bags next door, and left the rest of the mess to Matt's crew. Matt had a PFA crime scene crew there within the hour and they processed the entire room very quickly.

"We'll put a rush on this," Matt said, "Normally, we have all of the hotel staff on file . . . prints and other data, so we can eliminate them very quickly. If we find an odd print of somebody local, we'll have him nailed down pretty quick." Most of the time he was on his phone to somebody at the office, emphasizing the importance of the samples they were collecting. As it worked out, the samples were delivered and processed before they even left the room, which was almost five o'clock in the morning.

"Wow! That was fast" said Jake as Matt showed him the results on his phone.

"Well, that confirms it . . . the main suspect is a local thug for hire/burglar called Pedro Vasquez. He runs a little gambling operation in the San Telmo district. We don't usually have any problems with him, I think this time he just got sloppy." He paused and then added "It would be interesting to learn who put him up to this . . . this kind of thing is not his normal method of operation. Normally, like any good burglar, he's in and out without a fuss, no obvious clues, etc.. This job was almost like an amateur."

It was almost six when they agreed that nobody was going to get any sleep that night. "I suggest we all head down and get an early breakfast." said Elena. "We have something else we want to discuss with you two" as she pointed to Jake and Sabrina.

§

As they enjoyed their breakfast and multiple cups of coffee, Matt and Elena changed the subject and looked across to Sabrina and Jake. "O.K. you guys . . . here's what's going to happen!" Elena took over the conversation, not allowing any interruptions. "You are going to check out of the hotel, so it will appear that you heeded this guy's warning,"

"O.K., but we'll have to find another place that wouldn't be obvious that we haven't left town." said Jake.

"That's the best part" continued Elena, "we're heading out to my folks' place in the country, my parents' estancia. You'll love it, I guarantee, and you'll be safe, a lot safer than here in town!"

Matt interrupted at that point to add "And the best part is . . . nobody will know where you are, at least none of the 'bad guys'".

Jake and Sabrina agreed "That sounds good, Matt and Elena, peace and anonymity sounds really good right now."

"You've mentioned this 'estancia' a few times Elena, mainly when we were talking about food, about the 'Asado' barbecues, you have there. Please tell us more," asked Sabrina.

That was all Elena needed to open up about her parent's ancestral ranch she was so proud of. As it happened, the name of the ranch or *Estancia,* was 'Santa Elena', renamed after a change in the main use of the ranch. Several years before, her parents had decided to concentrate on the tourism industry rather than the cattle industry. It took fewer people to run the place, and they were not involved in all the politics related to raising cattle for food. So they decided to open a traditional hotel or lodge for tourists to book for vacations, sort of an up-scale B&B. They still raised some cattle and other animals, but mainly to add to the 'authentic Gaucho' experience. It was located in the pampas, about one hundred kilometres north of Buenos Aires, just beyond the town of San Antonio de Areco. This small town was a virtual 'tourist magnet', attracting visitors from Buenos Aires, to enjoy an authentic Argentine *Gaucho*, cowboy experience.

"Come on guys, let's get out of here." said Jake, as he paid for the meal and headed to the front desk to check out.

Matt interrupted them. "Hold it Jake, you guys still have your bags upstairs, and we don't even have ours. Why don't you get your stuff, have a shower, or whatever, and we'll pick you up later. Elena is going to run home and pack a bag for both of us. I have to stop by my office for something. We'll meet you back here within the hour, then we'll head out."

"Sounds good," Jake agreed, "I'm sure we can find something to fill our time for an hour or so."

§

Pedro Vasquez had been keeping track of the activities in the hotel most of the night. He was a little puzzled when no police cars showed up right away after the Prescotts had returned to their room. Instead, their tall friend and his wife who had been with them for dinner returned. Eventually, another van pulled up and a crime scene crew entered the hotel. Pedro had seen these guys in action before, but was surprised at the calm, quiet manner in which they operated this time. He was convinced the hotel staff had no idea what was going on. This piqued his curiosity even more, so he settled down in his car and watched. He decided that Prescott's friend must be a cop, from they way he moved and the way the entire operation had been handled. He started to worry about whether he had left any discriminating clues, anything to tie him to the crime.

He was looking forward to collecting his substantial 'fee' that Danko had promised, but he began to worry that this Prescott guy might not be the easy target he thought. What happens if he doesn't leave? How come he has a cop friend? There were too many loose ends, too many questions. He knew Danko was a crazy, hard nosed Serb, and he did not want to screw up. Fearing what Danko might do if he did fail, he started to think about the next step he had to take.

He was starting to feel hungry, wondering if he should take a chance and enter the hotel for some breakfast or walk down the street to one of the other bistro cafes. He hadn't decided when a few minutes later his waiting paid off. The cop-friend and his wife finally left the hotel, obviously finished with the event. Not long after, Prescott came out and slowly walked across to the park with his cane. His girlfriend was with him and they both and headed towards the cemetery. They had some brochures and a tourist map of the area in their hands, obviously out to explore the cemetery. At first, he couldn't understand why they were still here . . . why weren't they checking out and heading for the airport? Obviously his warning to go home wasn't enough. All he could think of was Danko would not like this. He tried to think what he was going to do next, what would scare a man like this, especially since he had a lovely wife, someone to protect.

§

Jake and Sabrina looked around, enjoying the sunlit park, beautiful gardens, lush green lawns and the spectacular selection of tall trees at the entrance to the famous Recoleta Cemetery. After their tiring and nerve racking night, they enjoyed the fresh, cool air of the park and decided this was great way to kill an hour or so until Matt and Elena returned to pick them up. Referring to their tourist information brochures they brought, they approached the main entrance, and were soon swallowed up by the incredible collection of gravestones, monuments and elaborate crypts.

It was like walking along strange streets or alleys, between tall buildings, a fantastic collection of monuments, from basic gravestones with short verses, to elaborate, huge mausoleums, usually topped with a crucifix, angel or some other religious figure. They found it fascinating, but difficult to see it all as they continued through the walkways, in some areas tall stone walls or crypts towering above them. Jake tried to translate some of the inscriptions for Sabrina as they went. A few other early morning tourists were also browsing the scene.

Pedro carefully followed the two, trying to stay out of sight in the adjacent 'street', wondering what he should do. As he moved quietly along, he also spotted the figures on the tops of the monuments, and an idea started to form in his head. Looking around, he spotted a long pruning wand used by the landscape people. "Just what I need" he thought, as the idea became a plan.

Jake and Sabrina had almost spent the hour they were trying to kill, but were glad they had fitted this little tour of the cemetery into their time. As they turned around a corner to return to the entrance, a noise above him caused Jake to jump back. He dropped his cane and grabbed Sabrina, pulling her back towards him as a large object crashed down from above. An elaborate cast figure of an angel, complete with outstretched wings, bounced off another tomb and smashed down in front of them, exploding into a thousand pieces.

"Jesus! What the hell?" yelled Jake, as Sabrina released herself from his grip. Before he could react, she was around the corner and running down another 'street', obviously in pursuit of a man Jake had not even noticed. The man ducked down another alley, hiding behind some tall tombstones of another monument. Sabrina was not fooled, she feinted a runaround, then doubled back just as the man tried to escape. Within seconds, she had caught and pulled the man down on the ground, quickly disabling him with an arm and choke hold.

The man sputtered in surprise, *"Madre de Dios...qué?"*... not expecting this kind of response from this sexy looking girlfriend.

As Jake caught up to Sabrina, he had figured out what had happened, and Sabrina had reacted much faster than he.

"Call Matt" she commanded Jake as he approached. "I want to know who this guy is and if he was the one who trashed our room."

Jake already had his phone out, and was soon talking with Matt. "We're almost there Jake . . . remember, we were coming back to pick you up. Don't tell me you guys got into some trouble just since we left you?"

"Not only that Matt, but Sabrina thinks she just caught the guy who trashed our room earlier."

# Vengeance - Chapter - 12

Matt and Elena were there within minutes. Matt was out of the car almost before it had stopped and leaving Elena in the car, headed towards the cemetery at a run where Jake and Sabrina were waiting with their captive. Matt couldn't believe what he saw as he approached the pair. Totally cool and controlled, Sabrina handed over a very subdued Pedro, who appeared to be still in shock at what happened.

Matt locked some handcuffs onto the man and looked at Sabrina with admiration. "Wow Jake! I can see now why you love this woman, she's a good one to have around if you run into any bad guys. Wait until I talk to Jacques in Lyon! He's told me she was a 'femme fatal', after that little episode in Bregenz last year." Both Jake and Sabrina were laughing now, but very relieved and glad it was over. "You were right Jake, or Sabrina. Let me introduce Señor Pedro Vasquez, small time crook and 'go-fer'."

Sabrina was pleased with her own insight into the matter. She realized that the attack in the cemetery was just a reinforcement of the warning they received in their hotel room. Her experience in law enforcement and criminal studies made her better equipped than Jake, even though his overall knowledge and reasoning ability still over-shadowed hers.

Elena walked over and interrupted at that point. She suggested "Come on guys, let's get out of here! Matt, hand that piece of shit over to one of your buddies here and let's go. I'm sure they will find out who's behind all this."

"I'd like to Elena, but we have a little paper-work to attend to first. Jake and Sabrina, you come with us now, we'll stop by headquarters for a few minutes to answer some questions. There are some people back there that are very interested in why this happened, and who was behind it." He shook his head, and added "then, then we'll get the hell out of town. Would you believe I had actually booked off today . . . didn't realize you guys were going to remain active" he laughed.

§

As they drove through Buenos Aires, Elena gave them a running 'tourist guide' commentary on everything they had passed, and pointed out all the spectacular buildings that had been built by the 'cattle barons' of old. Soon, they had finished their business at Matt's office and were ready to leave the city and experience the *Pampas*.

Matt headed out of town, northwest on Highway 8 and followed the Río Paraná for a short time towards the village of San Antonio de Areco. As Matt drove, the rest of them talked about the whole event, from the hotel break-in to the 'attack' at the cemetery. They were all convinced that Pedro had purposely tried to injure them by tipping over that statue, but they did not figure he was smart enough to realize the consequences if he had been successful. Either severe injury or death of a Canadian or Swiss tourist might have opened an entire 'can of worms' in the case. They knew he was hired to just scare them, convince them to go home, but this could have ended differently. Matt figured the guy was going to be in a lot of trouble when he tried to explain what happened. When they left the office, they had just started to question him, so maybe they could find out who hired him and why.

The answer came much faster than they expected. Matt's phone rang and he pushed a button to link the call to the car's speaker system. "*Hola Mateo? Eres tu?* Hello Matt, is that you?"

"Si Tomas, go ahead . . . what have you learned?"

"Well, you might be surprised at this . . . it also helps with that other case you're working on."

"What other case . . . what did you learn?"

"Remember the guy we tagged with the facial recognition thing?"

"Yeah, the Serbian guy who was supposed to be dead?"

"Yes, that's him, Danko Dragonović. He's the guy who hired this Pedro Vasquez . . . he was just supposed to scare Prescott . . . get him to leave town."

"So what else did you learn, where is this Danko character?"

"He works as a bouncer at a Milonga bar in the San Telmo district. It's called the *La Bebida Fuerte*."

Matt turned to Jake and the rest of them in the car. "See . . . I told you there was a connection . . . this is just too many coincidences happening at the same time." Turning his attention back to his call he added "OK Tomas, maybe let him go for now, with a warning not to mention any of this to Danko."

"But how is he going to explain all this?"

"That's his problem, he better just say he managed to accomplish only part of the job, but got interrupted, or something. But I want somebody on this Danko character . . . I want to know exactly where he is 24/7."

As he hung up the phone, Jake leaned across to him and said "Jesus Matt . . . it's that damn Serbian bitch again. She's behind this sure as hell!"

"I'm afraid you're right Jake. I'll call Jacques at Lyon to bring him up to speed as soon as we get to Elena's place . . . much easier than doing it from the car."

They all remained silent with their own thoughts as they carried on past the turnoff to San Antonio de Areco and continued on the main highway. Before long, he turned the car on to a side road and within minutes was pulling into a long driveway, lined with tall trees on both sides, heading up to a beautiful classic colonial house, standing majestically between two giant *Ombú* trees, symbols of the *Pampas*.

Elena turned to her two 'tourists' and said "Welcome to Estancia Elena . . . my home . . . and your home for your visit in Argentina."

# Vengeance - Chapter - 13

Franco Martinez had always been a good salesman. Even as a child in Spain, he learned how to convince other children to go along with him, or even surrender certain items to him. His relationship with his parents was based on a customer/salesman basis. He almost always managed to talk his way out of situations, convince his parents that 'he didn't do it', which left his siblings to take the blame. So, as he passed through school, he could talk his way into or out of any situation he wanted.

Of course his stature and overall demeanour helped. Franco was tall with an athletic frame, dark hair and striking dark brown eyes. When he entered a room, he took command, people tended to look to him for guidance, and generally believed anything he said. As a salesman, this was definitely an asset.

When his parents moved to California in the United states, he attended university and managed to expand his fluency in English. Some people with these manipulation skills are called 'con-men', with very little concern for others. Franco was the opposite, he managed to control others or change the conditions to benefit both himself and others involved, which probably was one of the reasons he was such a good salesman. He would always come out on top, but he never did anything to hurt another person or group.

But lately, he was experiencing what he could only describe as pangs of conscience It was the only time that he could remember when he had doubts about what he was doing He was aware of all the backlash and public critiques about his methods of operation. He wrote his own speeches, and he was the only one who could deliver them to an audience with force and impact that could fire up a crowd the way he did. He reasoned that as long as what he said was true, no matter how far-fetched it sounded, he was OK. In this case in Buenos Aires, the farming industry, particularly the cattle industry was under fire from what he called 'radical' environmental groups. There was a long list of environmental activists, 'tree huggers' and other do-gooders. There names were recognizable . . . usually an acronym or combination of feel good words or phrases. Many of the old favourites like GreenPeace, Earth-first, Sierra Club, Friends of the Earth, Nature Conservancy, made appearances from time to time, putting pressure on companies, governments and other organizations to change what they claimed to be destructive activities that were harmful to the environment and that threatened the future of mankind. It was either their agricultural methods they attacked, or it was the meat itself . . . claims that red meat increased the occurrence of colorectal, breast and prostate cancers. Then came the environmental impact . . .they claimed it was hurting the rain forests, too many trees were being cut for the farms to be planted, too many cattle were slaughtered inhumanely to provide meat for humans. The list grows on, so a consortium of cattle growers had approached his company, X-Sells, to convince the powers that be, the government, and any other protest groups, as well as the public at large that they needed farms, they needed agriculture, they needed the cattle industry. He quoted scientific studies that showed that more grassland, more pampas was beneficial to the environment, so the destruction of the forests was a good thing. He quoted other 'experts' that claimed the grass-fed beef was a healthy alternative to corn-fed beef, processed meats and meat substitutes, less fat, less cholesterol, less salt. It all sounded good to him, sounded like it was based on solid scientific principles and legitimate studies.

His meetings with his clients, representatives of the agriculture industry, sometimes confused him, which he knew was not good, he knew he must have a clear target in his mind, a clear idea of what he was trying to convince other people of, otherwise he could not do his job efficiently.

He had only been in Argentina for three months, but already he could feel himself coming under her spell . . . he was falling in love with a country! His memories of Spain had long since faded after the years he spent growing up with his parents in California. The years in California, at university, his first jobs, they all seem so unimportant now, just a training ground for the 'real world', the world of Argentina. Since the first day he arrived, he felt the pulse of the country through its music and dance in San Telmo, was dazzled by the multicoloured buildings of La Boca, the weekend markets, Plaza Serrano, the barrios and speakeasies of Palermo, awed by the majesty and solitude of the Recoleta Cemetery, all with his thirst and hunger more than satisfied by the incredible wines and the ubiquitous *asado*. He had began to feel it was even better than the wines and barbecues he enjoyed in California. He had developed a taste for the *yerba mate* that everyone drank in place of his normal coffee habit. He even learned to enjoy it like the locals or *portenos* to appreciate the drink sucked through a straw, sometimes a metal straw, rather than just drinking it out of a cup. On his infrequent days off, he would drive out into the country, just to experience the expanse of the *Pampas* and the majestic Ombú trees.

He had been shocked by the death of his opponent Tomas Romero at the last environmental protest meeting. At first he heard it was a heart attack, which did not surprise him as these events were super charged with emotion, so he could only feel sorry for the man and his family. The next day, he started hearing rumours that it might not have been a natural heart attack, but one brought on by artificial or man-made methods . . . in other words, murder!

§

As Jake and Sabrina followed Elena and Mateo into the *estancia,* they could not believe the size of the rooms, or the sheer beauty of the furnishings and decor. Antique chairs, tables and wall hangings surrounded them, carved wooden chairs with elaborate hand-tooled leather seats, classic Spanish colonial influence everywhere.

"Oh my God, Elena," exclaimed Sabrina, "It's all so beautiful . . .what a wonderful home!"

"Oh I'm so glad you like it . . . I only wish my parents were here to meet you. They're on a wine buying trip over in Mendoza this week, they'll be back soon." She waved her hands to include the entire room and added "Some of the tourists that stay here think it's too much . . . too many antiques, too 'old school'"

Sabrina laughed "Well, not me . . . you have to remember I am from Switzerland. Everywhere we go we see antiques, old architecture, and like you said, a lot of 'old school' stuff."

Matt was dragging Jake off in another direction. "Come on Jake, let's go get a cold beer while we talk with one of my bosses in Lyon . . . Jacques Manet."

Jake agreed and before long they were each enjoying a beer while they caught Jacques in his Interpol office. Matt took over the first part of the conversation while he explained what had happened in the Recoleta Cemetery and how Sabrina had taken down the perpetrator in short order and held him until the police arrived. Jacques was delighted, and asked Matt to repeat several sections of the conversation.

"Bloody Hell Jake! She's done it again! If Sabrina wasn't already working for law enforcement, we'd hire her immediately!" Jake felt an intense feeling of pride for his girl, as they could feel Jacques' pleasure and excitement come over the phone, Sabrina had just cemented another brick into Jacques' wall of admiration for her.

"If I might interrupt this little admiration party for my girl-friend, Jacques" began Jake, can we talk about this Danko character? And his go-fer Pedro, the guy that broke into our room, the guy that you two are laughing about right now? What are these guys up to, are they being directed by our Serbian bitch?"

"Blimey, that's the question alright!" Jacques mused. Everything we've found so far points in that direction, except we don't know what her ultimate plan is, what is she trying to do? What have your people found down there Matt?"

Matt began to talk, and Jake could see that he was measuring his words, making sure everything he said made sense. "Well," he started, "First, we know that someone tampered with Tomas Romero's *mate* at that meeting. We're still not sure who, we only know what kind of poison it was . . . thanks to Jake's chemist in Vancouver." He paused, gathering his thoughts, and continued. "We know the protest meeting was a highly charged event, but nobody expected it to go that far. Second, we now know this Serbian guy Danko was sent here for a specific purpose . . . not sure what . . . but he's suddenly involved with trying to convince Jake and Sabrina to leave town. Again, we're not sure why." Matt stopped, then smiled and added "At least we know something about Danko, he works as a bouncer over in San Telmo at a Milonga bar there . . . that's where he made contact with Pedro, the small time crook you guys nabbed this morning."

"So," Jake said slowly, "We really don't know anything solid that we can use!" Jacques' voice came booming out over the speaker phone. "I might remind you Jake, that you and my girl Sabrina are supposed to be there on vacation. I would appreciate it if you could back off a little and let Mateo and his crew carry on with their investigations. You guys go and enjoy some of this 'vacation' time, go somewhere quiet and secluded and take real good care of her. I'd be very upset if she gets damaged in any way during all this messing about!"

Jake answered quickly "Well first of all Jacques, you should know that I haven't been doing anything, just trying to mind my own business. It's somebody else that's doing the 'messing about', not us. They are the ones causing the trouble. Anyway, you'll be pleased to know we have found the perfect 'hide-out' while we are in Buenos Aires. I'll let Matt tell you about where we are, and where we'll be for the foreseeable future."

# Vengeance - Chapter - 14

Jacques Manet was delighted with the recent phone call from Buenos Aires. His admiration of Sabrina had just increased by a hundredfold. But his concern for what was happening down there troubled him, and he knew he had to do something to change that. What the hell was that woman up to, thinking about the Serbian poison expert called Dr. Dejana Babić. He knew there were a lot of environmental protests going on in Argentina and Brazil, related to the destruction of the forests in the Amazon and the Argentine pampas, mainly to increase grazing land for more cattle. Recently, several environmental activist organizations had descended on Buenos Aires, all trying to become active in the protests against the agriculture industry. Jacques called his secretary, and asked "Annette, would you please ask Malina to drop by my office, and you come in as well. I have a project for both of you."

§

When Malina Aleksov arrived with Annette, she was worried. Her entire existence here at Interpol headquarters was tenuous, all subject to her success with maintaining her 'double agent' deception with Dejana Babić. She needn't have worried, as Jacques greeted her enthusiastically and had them both relax and sit down.

Jacques was the first to speak. "Malina, you said last time we talked that you were considering going home to visit family soon, taking a few days off. How are those plans progressing . . . have you anything planned?"

Malina suddenly felt better. She answered quickly "Yes, I am flying out to Beograd this weekend, staying at my aunt's place for a week."

"Does Dejana know you are coming?"

"Yes, she just asked me yesterday, so I will see her for a short visit while I'm there. Not much . . . maybe go out for lunch or something."

"Are you ready for that?" asked Jacques, glancing over to Annette, who had been informed of Malina's rôle in the entire affair.

"Oh yes," she answered. "I'm ready. I have several answers for her if she asks me certain questions, and I have some questions for her."

"Like what?"

"I think I'll ask her about Buenos Aires, nothing specific, I'll just say if I knew what she was looking for, I might be able to watch for communications that might help. I figure I might learn something that you could use."

"Right, good idea. Anything else you want to ask her?"

"Nothing specific, is there something you'd like me to say or ask?"

"No. I want anything between you and her to be as natural as possible . . . nothing that might make her suspicious, or sound like a question from me."

Annette interrupted at this point to add "And if there is anything you want to tell us . . . do not use our email address . . . I think she is monitoring some of them. Just drop a note to my address, like you were emailing a colleague or friend while you are on vacation. I think you know enough to make the message vague or nonsense to anyone else?"

"Yes, great Annette, I was wondering if there was a way I could do that."

As they ended the meeting, Jacques felt much better, and decided to ask Annette to monitor this little deception as closely as she could.

§

Meanwhile, Dejan Babić was boiling. As she sat in her office in her country laboratory, she had just received an email from Danko in Buenos Aires. Apparently his plan to scare Prescott and his girlfriend out of Buenos Aires had not worked . . in fact the person he hired to do the job had been arrested and had admitted who had hired him. So Dejana was stuck without a person in Buenos Aires. She knew she could not use Danko, he would be questioned and monitored. She knew he wouldn't give her up, he would die before releasing her name to the law. So what was she to do? She knew she had the X-Sells people on site . . . but they were a different sort of people . . . for the most part, they were scientists, salesmen, not strong-arm men or killers. If things get really desperate, she knew she had the option of calling in an old favour, but it involved bringing in undesirables from the narco-mafia, something she had tried to avoid all her years in business.

She weighed her options and decided on another option she hadn't yet tried. She had to do something . . . this contract was worth too much money to let drop . . . and the environmental nuts were swarming into Buenos Aires, putting on a lot of pressure. She had to come up with a solution, so she decided to activate one of her 'secret weapons'. With that decision made, she picked up the phone and dialed a number in California, USA.

A man answered, and they immediately switched their conversation to Serbian. After a lengthy conversation, he finally hung up the phone with a smile on his face. Closing his briefcase, he left his office, tossing back a brief comment to his secretary that he would be out of town for a while.

§

Dejana looked at her calendar and noticed that her distant niece, Malina Aleksov was coming to Beograd next weekend for a short vacation. A plan began to form as she decided to meet with this young spy of hers and increase her duties. She knew Malina's aunt, and saw her in Beograd periodically doing her shopping. She decided to call her and invite her to a luncheon date with Malina when she arrived. That accomplished, she already felt a little better.

§

Sabrina was enthralled with the home, from the clay tiles on the roof she spotted as they arrived, reminiscent of the homes in Italy or Spain, the beautiful polished marble floor tiles, alternating with glazed clay paving stones. The great room where they had entered first, enjoyed a massive stone fireplace at one end, topped with a huge timber for a mantle and wooden beams across the ceiling, supporting rough sawn planks that formed the floor above. It was all both familiar and strange together. She had seen many of these features in European homes, but this house had a different flavour to it, a soft, older flavour, a friendlier one. Once they had seen the main parts of the house, they were taken to their rooms, another delightful surprise. She was totally taken by the luxury, the beautiful furniture, and luxurious beds with thick duvets. Later, she made a point to find Jake and drag him away from Matt for a few minutes. "Oh Jake! This is so lovely, we're going to enjoy our stay here I'm sure." She spotted the worried look on Jake's face and added "And for you, you better stop plotting with Matt and try to relax. I'm sure he has a few ideas about what we should do while we're here."

"As a matter of fact, he already has made some suggestions... the first one is some practice on his shooting range."

"He's got a shooting range too?"

"Yes, of course, many ranches have a range where they can shoot, test their weapons, practice."

"Of course, so when are we going?"

"Right now! Matt and Elena are bringing out a selection of handguns and rifles to try, do you want to join us?"

"Of course, sounds like fun. Ask Elena to pick me up in the great room, I'm still admiring the decor."

§

They met again at a small shed behind from the house. Targets were mounted at ten metre intervals from the sheltered area at one end. Two long clotheslines installed for setting and retrieving targets, made recovering their targets very easy.

"Hi guys, are you ready to be beaten by a couple of female shooters?" started Elena as they arrived. "What do you say Sabrina? From what I've heard, you are a pretty good shot."

Sabrina reached into her handbag and pulled out a small handgun, barely larger than her hand.

"Wow! What's that?" Matt exclaimed. "What a little beauty!"

"It's my favourite travel gun, a little Baretta Pico, .38 calibre"

This brought on more questions both from Matt and Jake. Sabrina tried to explain "I already told Jake... I didn't take it on the plane, it was in my hold baggage... must I remind you that a law enforcement officer can get permission to own and carry a firearm under certain circumstances? That's something I wanted to talk to you about Matt, what are the rules in Argentina? After some of the things we've been going through, I think I'll be carrying it more often." She looked around at all the surprised looks. "OK, are we going to shoot or what?"

Matt laughed, "Why of course, but why bother with that little peashooter? Can it hit anything over six feet away?"

Sabrina answered him with a challenge. "I'll have you know this is a .38 calibre and quite deadly . . . and if you think you're so good, I challenge you to beat me. I'll use my little Pico, you use whatever you like."

"Done!" Matt jumped at the chance. "Challenge accepted". He knew his Argentine Bersa 'Thunder 9' was very accurate, almost always better than the usual Glock 17 the other officers used.

They all donned safety gear and Sabrina took position at one of the shooting locations at the counter. "OK Matt, you first, let's see what an Argentine police officer can do.

Matt stood up and fired off six rounds at his target. They pulled in the target and announced the results. "Not bad", said Sabrina, smiling. "Now I'll show you how a 'peashooter' does it," as she quickly fired six rounds from her weapon. Matt's face dropped slightly as she pulled in her target from the range.

"*Madre de Dios*!" he exclaimed as he saw the results. "How did you do that" he stammered, you beat me in every shot . . . with that little Pico. I've got to get one of those for Elena."

"I'm way ahead of you there Matt." said Elena, "I've already talked about this with Sabrina, and I'm going to order one right away."

They practiced for another hour, each one trying to beat Sabrina. At last, they gave up and decided it was time for drinks.

# Vengeance - Chapter - 15

The next few days were a dream for Sabrina and Jake. It was the vacation they had wished for, the one they had been planning for a long time, but didn't realize it would be this good. Elena was the prefect hostess, spoiling them by catering to their every need and desire. They basked in the enjoyment of being pampered in an authentic estancia, as the worries and concerns of the recent events faded from their consciousness.

Elena's housekeeper, Sofia, made sure they were well fed, from huge breakfasts to late-night snacks. Their hosts kept them entertained with excursions of the estate, horseback rides, gaucho music and stories, and evenings full of wine and delicious asado barbecues.

One day they ventured into San Antonio de Areco, the little village they had passed on the way to the estancia. The village was a goldmine of Argentine history, culture and the folklore of the gaucho. 'Gauchesco' souvenirs were everywhere, clothes, hats, leather work, and jewelry shops were all through the town. Sabrina enjoyed the shopping with Elena while Matt and Jake just browsed around between cold beers and calls from Matt's office. As it turned out, things were very quiet, nothing had changed, no major events or disasters had occurred.

They had heard nothing from Jacques at Interpol about what was happening in Serbia, and Matt had not received any alerts from his man Tomas in Buenos Aires. Jake checked with Peter in Vancouver periodically about any possible computer traffic going on, that too was quiet.

§

It was the following weekend when Elena's parents returned to the estancia. Elena patiently waited for them to enter the house so she could introduce them to her guests. As they came in the door, they hardly had time to take off their coats when Elena rushed over to them, embracing them both with kisses, the words tumbling out of her.

"*Whoa, Cariña, más lento, por favor!* Whoa, darling, slower, please." her father pleaded.

Elena backed up and turned to her friends. "Sabrina, Jake . . . may I introduce my parents, Paula and Nicolas Sanchez." Turning back to her parents, she added "This is Sabrina Wagner from Switzerland and Jake Prescott from Canada. Not only are they my friends, but they are our house guests for however long they decide to stay!"

Paula and Nicolas were delighted to meet their daughter's friends, and welcomed them to their home. As Jake shook Nicolas' hand, he could feel the callouses and strength of a man used to hard work. The man's face was smooth as a young man's, darkly tanned with a short, well trimmed white beard. Small creases in the corners of his dark eyes, gave testament to the outdoor work he did around the estancia.

"*Bienvenidos, w*elcome both of you to our home. We have had visitors from your countries before, but this is the first time Elena has brought home her friends to stay."

Oh Papá, we have so much to tell you about these two. Jake was at the university when Mateo and I were there . . . and . . ."

Her mother interrupted at this point. "Please, Cariña, could we come in and relax a moment before you begin your story . . . can we all meet for drinks on the patio and get to know each other? Your Papá has some new wine we picked up in Mendoza . . . he's dying to try it with everyone."

"Of course, Mamá, how stupid of me . . . I've been so excited for you to meet them! I'll ask Sofia to help us."

They all met again on their expansive patio, the warm breeze drifting in from the pampas. They were surrounded by gardens filled with flowering shrubs and tall trees. Nicolas brought out a couple of bottles of his new wines, some new vintages from his favourite vineyard of Mendoza. He was followed by Sofia, carrying a large tray of golden brown *empanadas,* an Argentine staple.

"I think you'll like these ones," Nicolas announced to the group as he opened the wine, "they are from an old friend of mine who owns a vineyard just outside of Mendoza. The grapes are Malbec, his vineyard is up in the Maipú area . . . it's up over a thousand metres . . . just under the Andes. You should see it . . . absolutely spectacular! They have a slightly different soil on a sunny slope . . . perfect for Malbec . . .well . . . try it and see."

"Nicolas!" his wife sharply interrupted . . ." just pour the wine! Let everyone try it . . . they don't need a lecture on it's provenance and terroir."

Nicolas laughed and said "Of course my dear, I just get a little carried away when I think of where this comes from." With that he poured everyone a large glass of a ruby red treat that sparkled in the late afternoon sun.

§

The rest of the afternoon was a treat for Sabrina and Jake . . . a dream vacation that had developed in a completely different way. The wine and Sofia's empanadas were a delight and so was the conversation with Paula and Nicolas. Jake and Sabrina were a star attraction for the couple, especially when they started recounting stories from Mateo's days at university, right up to some of the events of the day before. The hours wore on, until somebody remarked how late it was and how hungry they were.

With that, Nicolas jumped up and declared he was going to give them a treat . . . he loved cooking, and he was going to serve them his specialty from *la cocina,* the kitchen. "This is a historical old recipe handed down for generations," he announced. "'*Lasaña campestre',* it's a rural style lasagna with Swiss chard, ricotta, cooked ham and cheese. I think you'll enjoy it . . . especially if Mateo has been feeding you *asado* every meal . . . it's a nice change."

§

The meal was indeed a treat, and as Nicolas promised, a welcome change to the huge slabs of meat of the asado barbecues. They had barely finished their meal and were enjoying yet another glass of wine when Sofia came out and whispered something in Matt's ear. His demeanour turned serious and he left immediately, heading into the house. Jake noticed the move and followed shortly after, shooting a worried glance at Sabrina.

He saw Matt was on the house phone, listening intently to whatever was being said. He waited patiently until Matt stopped and hung up the phone. "What is it Matt . . . what was that all about?" fearing the worse.

Matt turned, a worried look on his face. "That damn bitch . . . she's got longer arms than we suspected."

"What Matt, what happened?"

"Your burglar . . . Señor Vasquez . . . was just found dead, just outside a bar in San Telmo. Witnesses said he got into an argument with some tough looking guy . . . that's all they have so far."

"You think it was our Serbian guy, the guy you suspected of hiring him?"

"That's what it looks like, but the guys in the office aren't too concerned. They figure it's just one less criminal on the street."

"That's good isn't it?" Jake asked.

"Yes and no. We were hoping we could have used him, you know, he's our only link back to the bitch. I doubt if we'll get anything out of Danko, he's probably too smart to leave any clues around."

# Vengeance - Chapter - 16

Malina's aunt picked her up at the Nicola Tesla Airport in Beograd and drove her straight to their home. Malina smiled each time she flew home and used this airport, mainly because of the international attention that the name 'Nicola Tesla' commanded in recent years. All her life, she had grown up familiar with the work of Nicola Tesla and the fantastic inventions and ideas that he had produced, only to lose them in unwise business arrangements. Most people in modern times think of electric cars, or space vehicles when they hear that name, not realizing that the electrical power delivered to their houses and offices, the lighting, and even the internet was made possible by the ideas and inventions of Nicola Tesla. Ideas like wireless power transmission, remote control submarines, and monstrous lightning bolts were part of his heritage.

Malina had a good visit for a couple of days with her aunt, but she was looking forward to the luncheon date with Dejana. Her aunt knew Dejana, but only slightly from the occasional 'work bonuses' she received in the mail for Malina's work, bonuses she didn't quite understand as Malina worked for Interpol, not Dejana Babić Malina had told her that these were for an additional part-time job she had, and not to worry about it. Her aunt was smart enough to drop the subject and not pursue it any further.

She was surprised Malina told her she had a luncheon date with the woman. "I've talked to her a few times about my work" Malina said cautiously, "She seemed proud that a member of the family was working with Interpol."

"Well that is so nice you are going to see her again. I heard that one of her employees was killed in Austria last year."

"Yes, she mentioned that. We'll probably be talking about it more today."

They met on the side of the Republika Square, a huge clear square in Beograd, ringed with sidewalk restaurants. On one side of the square was a large bronze statue of Prince Mihailo, or Prince Michael, astride his horse. The statue, by Italian sculptor Enrico Pazzi, was erected in honour of Prince Michael's achievement of the complete expulsion of the Turks from Serbia in 1867. In modern times, the square was a favourite meeting place for many people, and an easy place to find.

Dejana was already seated at one of the little cafes on one side of the square, across from Prince Michael. She spotted Malina as soon as she entered the square, and beckoned her over. After a brief greeting and exchange of social niceties, they sat and ordered coffees.

Dejana started first. "I'm so glad we could get together. How was your flight, how is your aunt?"

Malina felt uncomfortable at first, but then reminded herself that she was OK, she hadn't done anything wrong, she had nothing to worry about, so she became more social, a little more aggressive. "I don't know exactly what's going on in Buenos Aires, but since I sent that last bit of information to you about Prescott's hotel, there has been a lot of traffic, emails and calls back and forth."

"About what?" Dejana asked. "Do you know what is going on?"

"Only that there was a problem at the hotel, and somebody was arrested, I don't know who." Malina did know, but was not going to give Dejana the name without getting something in return. Before she had a chance to say anything more, Dejana interrupted.

"Malina . . . I've been meaning to ask you. Remember last year, I gave you a small vial of something to put in your boss's coffee. Do you still have that?"

"Oh my goodness no . . . things were too busy and scary at that time, I couldn't do anything that would appear suspicious, so I threw it out. Don't you remember, all that activity in Bregenz?"

"Yes, yes, that was a bad time." Dejana certainly did remember . . . a very bad time for her. She continued "I thought that was what might have happened, so I have another job for you. Would you please listen for anything about the company called X-Sells. I just would like to know if they are talking about them or if anything is happening I should know." She hesitated then added "Here is another vial . . . just keep it safe . . . no need to use it now. If there is a need for it later, I will let you know." She noticed a bit of concern on Malina's face. "And I think your aunt should get a bonus for her nieces, just to make things more comfortable for her."

Malina had hoped an extra payment would be offered, even if she hadn't poisoned her boss as she was told. Her mind was in a turmoil, and other thoughts began to go through her mind as another plan began to form. She smiled at the thought, and almost gave herself away.

"What?" said Dejana . . ." is something amusing . . . you smiled just then?"

"No, no, I am so glad you can send some extra money for the nieces, they are so special to her and to me. Thank you."

"Fine. Is there anything extra you want to discuss?"

"Not specifically, but I was wondering . . . is there was anything you wanted, anything you want me to watch for . . . I can keep my eyes open in case something comes my way."

"Oh, actually, that's a good idea . . . I'll keep it in mind, just remember the name X-Sells, and I'll let you know if I need anything else."

Just before they parted, Malina's idea had formed in her mind as she pocketed the small vial, an idea for her long term security. As she said goodbye, she added "I enjoyed our little meeting . . . I find it much better to talk face to face. We'll have to do this again some day."

"Of course Malina, of course."

§

Franco Martinez was becoming more concerned. He was not aware of the other activities of the police at Recoleta, but he certainly had noticed the high energy investigation that had taken place after Tomas Romero had died at the conference. Not only died, but from what he heard, was murdered. Who could be responsible for such a thing? It wasn't long before the police asked him to answer a few questions, after all, they had been on opposite sides of the fence during the conference, and he was considered as a rival or opponent of the politician.

The questioning took place in the police headquarters, nothing specific, just a general inquiry about their 'relationship', etc., and other matters. Franco had very little information he could offer, as he had only arrived on the scene a few months ago and did not even know Tomas Romero before the rally. He only knew that he had to keep his wits about him, somebody was obviously getting serious about the matters they were debating.

# Vengeance - Chapter - 17

Matt and Jake talked about the latest development for the next hour or two. Neither one was surprised at Señor Vasquez' fate, but they were a little taken aback at the speed at which it had happened. Whoever was behind it, appeared to be very impatient, not wanting to waste time in getting things done. Things like disposing of anyone who gets in the way, or anyone who slows them down. Matt's crew were still trying to find Danko, the man they suspected was Dr. Babić's local muscle. They knew he had been working at a bar in San Telmo, but ever since Vasquez had shown up dead, he had not been to work, and nobody knew where he was.

§

Danko knew they were looking for him, and he was trying his best not to be found. That damn Vasquez, the idiot went too far with the Prescotts. . . he was just supposed to scare them, not try to kill them! He caught up with him shortly after he was released, and learned what had happened, how he had been taken down by that wild cat woman with Prescott. "God, she was fast!" he moaned, "and deadly . . . had me down before I even knew she was there"

"But why were you even there? What were you trying to do?" Danko asked. "You were only supposed to scare them, try to convince them to go home."

The answers he received were not reassuring. The idiot obviously did not have the experience or street smarts that Danko originally thought he did. While they were talking, the idiot started explaining to Danko how he would make it up, how he would 'get them ' next time. It was too much . . . he had seen these types before, he would not be able to convince him to back off . . . to leave it alone. No matter what he did, things would just get worse. So Danko just did what he always did when he had a problem . . . remove it!

Unfortunately, that just made the problem worse. Danko was not used to the tight policing in the neighbourhood. The police had found the body even before he had returned home. He blamed himself, he shouldn't have left things so loose and obvious. Buenos Aires was different from the cities in Serbia or Bosnia that he knew. If people here saw something the least bit suspicious, they called the cops. He thought that the body would stay 'lost' in that alley for days, maybe a week before somebody found it. As he approached his apartment complex, he saw the flashing lights of the PFA in front of the building and asked the taxi to go around the block. At first he wondered why they were after him, then he realized that Vasquez had probably told them everything . . . that he had been hired by Danko. All Vasquez' talk about 'getting even', or 'finishing the job' was bullshit. The bastard had told the police everything they needed to know to put it all together and come after him.

Once again, he had to disappear. He directed the taxi to head out of town closer to the river, and started searching for a place to rent. With the help of the taxi driver, he managed to find a small flat, rented it under a different name, cash payment, no questions asked. With no luggage or extra clothes, he settled in and tried to make plans on what to do next. If he was going to hide out and figure out his next move, he needed food, booze, clothes, and if he were lucky, women.

§

Franco started asking around about the Tomas Romero thing. Does anyone know why he was killed? Who would do such a thing? What was the reason? All these questions remained unanswered, at least to him. It sounded like there were others who did know something, but were not telling. He kept asking questions, sometimes to the point of getting others angry. "What the hell do you want to know that for?" "Why don't you ask . . .?" But he did not give up, he was determined to find out, mainly because he did not want to be associated with any group or organization involved in the murder of an opponent, he wanted nothing to do with it, so he decided he would find out just who was responsible. He was not a detective, and had no experience at this, but he did have an analytical mind, a mind that puts things together. Even in school and university, he could assemble unrelated facts and deduce a solution, a reasonable solution to the problem.

First, from what he knew, a murderer had to have a motive. Why did he do it? Whoever was responsible was most likely opposed to Romero's stand. So who wanted to stop Romero? The country was full of environmental activists and 'tree hugger' groups who wanted to shut down everything for the sake of 'the environment'. He had seen it everywhere . . . the USA and Canada, as well as many countries in Europe were filled with such organizations. Usually they just protested with marches, signs and large gatherings, but rarely resorted to violence, especially on a scale like this.

It was his job to oppose these groups and convince others that what the agriculture industry was doing was not that bad. In fact it was he, Franco Martinez that was the most obvious one that wanted to get rid of Romero. No wonder he was brought in for questioning. He hadn't seen the connection before, but it became clear once he connected the dots. X-Sells had only a small staff in Buenos Aires, mainly secretaries and an office manager to keep things alive. So he was the main suspect that had a motive to dispose of Romero. He realized he must change that and started to analyze everyone's connection to the project.

He then took it up one more level. Who had hired X-Sells to come to Buenos Aires and argue the case? The answer was obvious, the various agriculture consortiums in Argentina and Brazil . . . the same ones who were getting the static about farmland versus forests, animal versus plant agriculture, meat versus vegetables. It was big business, lots of money, a lot to lose if things went the wrong way. So . . . who else have they hired? Surely he was not the only player in a game this big. Was X-Sells the only company involved, or were there others in the mix? He pondered this question and it wasn't until he started looking at the company itself that he got his first clue. Looking at some of the company information from when he was hired, he noticed a little detail that triggered memories from several months ago. X-Sells' parent company was a Serbian company run by a woman botanist chemist. It was this little bit of data that triggered his memory . . . a mention of a Serbian man who was killed in a bizarre encounter in Austria the previous summer. After 'Googling' the information, he learned more of the details, and was satisfied it was the same company involved. He decided he would have to ask some more questions. The first place he decided to ask questions was the police. In Buenos Aires it was the PFA, the Policia Federal Argentine. He phoned and asked for whoever was investigating the Tomas Romero murder. There was a long pause on the phone . . . then a man answered and immediately asked "What makes you assume it was murder?"

He was slightly taken aback, not expecting this kind of response. He quickly gathered his wits and asked "Are you the officer in charge of the Romero investigation?"

"That depends . . . who is asking, and what is your interest in the case? Are you a relative of Señor Romero?"

Franco backed off, realizing how he must sound to the police officer. "No, No, I'm sorry, I should have identified myself first. My name is Franco Martinez, I was at the rally where Romero was killed . . . I say killed, because that is what's going around on social media. They figure he was too young for a heart attack, but then you would know. I've already been questioned by your people, I think mainly because I was his opponent in the argument . . . public debate." He stopped, gathering his thoughts for the next step. "Can I speak to the officer in charge of the case?"

"Do you have some new information? Why do you want to talk to him?"

"I just have a few ideas, a few things that might add some light to his investigation, I know something about some other people involved that he might be interested in."

"OK, I have your name, give me your contact phone number and I'll have him call you as soon as he returns."

"Returns?"

"Yes, he's out of town just now, but I'll try to contact him."

# Vengeance - Chapter - 18

Mateo Perez received a call from his PFA office, one that stimulated his interest. "Jake . . . I just got a call . . . some guy wants to talk to me about the Romero case. Says he has some information I might be interested in . . . something about another guy at the meeting where Romero died."

"Did he give you any more than that, 'another guy'?"

"No, but his name is Franco Martinez, one of the the main opponents of Romero on this environment thing. He runs the local office of X-sells. I think we should talk to him."

"We . . .?"

"Of course! You're involved in this thing as much as I am, even though you're not officially a police officer, I need you to sit in on the interrogation as a 'consultant', because of your clever mind, Prescott."

Jake laughed, mainly because he was hoping to be included in any further investigations. He was curious about all the connections and his mind was already starting to form a picture of what was happening. "So tell me Matt, what is going on right now in Buenos Aires . . . how come all these environmental activists and enviro-politicians are duking it out here now? I try to keep track of any conferences going on around the world, and this isn't one."

"Well, not really an environmental conference like you are used to Jake, but it is an important gathering all the same."

"What kind of 'gathering'".

"A gathering of all the so-called 'green organizations' to work together to put up a united front against firms or industries . . . or even countries to do something about their 'greenhouse gas emissions' and their 'carbon footprint', I think it's called."

"So why Argentina . . . why Buenos Aires . . . why now?"

"I don't know Jake. you're the expert, you tell me. Argentina right now is large enough to make a huge impact, yet a little smaller than Brazil to tackle in this argument. It's the first time we've seen a lot of these environmental groups work together to put pressure on a country. Outfits like Greenpeace, Sierra Club, Environmental Defence Fund, and others . . . they all usually just make their own case. Apparently, somebody decided they should join forces and put on a combined attack. So . . . here we are . . . almost in the middle of 'ground zero', so to speak."

Jake absorbed that information, nodding his head. "I've been thinking Matt . . . trying to figure out what else might be happening here. With these two political opponents, or activists, and all these guys screaming for 'the environment' . . . the entire thing sounds very familiar."

"In what way?" asked Matt.

"Well, in Europe, there wasn't an obvious set of opponents like here . . . but the situation is similar. Somebody is trying to eliminate anyone who is trying to reveal the problems of global warming. So far, you only have one fatality, and one collateral victim."

"Well," said Matt, thinking seriously about what Jake was saying "As far as we know."

Jake asked about their planned meeting with Franco Martinez. "So when is this event?"

"We're heading into town first thing in the morning. Tomas, my right-hand man in the office, is going to try to have that guy there at eleven o'clock."

§

Franco was a little surprised when he received a call to show up at the police office at eleven the next morning. He had nothing important to do, and he really wanted to get this off his mind.

As he entered the building, a tall man greeted him, Officer Perez, an imposing figure of authority, a man he wouldn't want to argue with on any subject. He was introduced to another tall man with a cane, described as a consultant in the case. At first, Matt talked to him in Spanish, then switched to English. "I understand you speak English as well, so if you don't mind, we'll use that language for this interview for the benefit of Mr. Prescott."

"No problem, English is fine with me."

They made sure Franco was seated comfortably and started the discussion with "Well, Señor Martinez, what do you have to tell us? You asked for this opportunity to give us some information you considered important. Please continue"

Franco was a little surprised, but also pleased they had taken him seriously. He started with "Well, I think it could be important, but you might not think so . . . I was just putting together some . . ."

"Why don't you just tell us what you are thinking . . . let us determine if it fits into our investigation."

So Franco started with his suspicions that somebody must have slipped something into Romero's drink at the meeting, and as he was the obvious opponent present, of course he was questioned. He suspected that it went deeper than himself, his company, X-Sells was part of a Serbian company run by a Serbian woman who was an expert in poisons, who he remembered was involved in the situation in Austria the previous year. He wasn't sure, but he felt it was linked somehow, and they should know about it.

Matt looked over at Jake and smiled, both thinking the same thing. "Well, Señor Martinez, we appreciate your concerns, and your suspicions." started Matt. "We have already connected those dots, and have moved on a little further. Have you any additional information you could provide?"

Franco was a little surprised, but then thought 'Of course, they are experts at this'. He was trying to think what else was bothering him, what else can he tell these men? Before he had a chance to think of something, they asked "Would you mind telling us, Señor Martinez, who is your boss . . . your immediate superior?"

The question surprised him a little, but it was not unusual or any secret. "My boss is in California actually . . . that's where the head office of X-Sells is. His name is Ray Marko . . . I've only met him a couple of times after I was hired. Why do you ask?"

"Just for information Franco, do you mind if we call you Franco?"

"No problem, that's my name."

Matt asked a few questions in Spanish and got the answers he expected . . . in precise Castilian Spanish, or 'Castellano' Spanish, complete with the soft pronunciation of certain consonants, almost a lisp sound. Even Jake, who was not fluent in Spanish, detected the differences.

"Thank you Franco, we appreciate you coming in today, and appreciate your concern about the matter of Tomas Romero's death. I'm sure our investigation will figure it all out eventually. Could you please leave some contact information with my secretary at the front, just in case we'd like to talk to you again.

In the meantime, here is my card . . . in case you think of anything more you'd like to discuss."

The session finished, Franco left, and Matt and Jake looked at each other, each waiting for the other to comment.

"I don't know Jake. I've got a funny feeling about all this. This Franco seems like a nice guy, but I think I'll ask Jacques' people at Interpol to look at both him and his boss . . . this Ray Marko."

Jake replied with a nod. "Yes, definitely, especially as we know who the parent company is . . . I'd like to know if there are any more connections."

Matt immediately asked his secretary to place an inquiry to Interpol Lyon, to check on Mr. Marko and further information on X-Sells.

§

They had not even left the office when Matt's phone rang. He answered quickly as he did not recognize the number. "Yes? Oh yes Franco, no, no . . . no trouble at all" He frantically gestured to Jake to stay. "What can I help you with?"

As he continued with the call, it was mainly listening, slowly nodding his head. "OK, great Franco, and thank you so much for calling, I'll make a note of that."

As he hung up, he turned to Jake. "Well, that's interesting. Apparently Mr. Ray Marko is coming to Buenos Aires in a couple of days, wants to 'check on things' and provide any help that Franco might need."

"Interesting indeed . . . what has changed . . . why is the 'big boss' coming? I'm sure it's not just to 'check on things'. When do you expect an answer from Jacques?"

"I'll put a rush on it, should have something before tomorrow, depends on how deep they have to dig."

§

Back at the estancia, they enjoyed another huge meal and an evening of wonderful stories told by Elena's mother and father, mainly recounting stories from their past, stories their parents told them. Matt couldn't tell them much about their trip into town, there wasn't much to tell. Both Matt and Jake were anxious to receive word back from Lyon, even though they had very few reasons to create any anxiety.

Once they were alone, Sabrina wanted to know every detail, every word that was spoken, until she had the entire picture, and she too was waiting anxiously for answers from Lyon . . . if there were any. After showering, they slipped on soft bathrobes and shared some wine on their balcony. They could feel the soft breezes drifting from the pampas, filled with aromas of grassland, blossoms and the sweet smell of new-mown hay in the small pasture nearby. Sabrina leaned over to Jake, her bathrobe slipping down a little too low, exposing one of her breasts. "I missed you today Jake." she said plaintively. "I had a lot of fun with Elena, but it's not the same without you."

Jake's body was quick to respond to the exposed skin. His thoughts were more on Sabrina than his day, but he tried to answer "Oh Sabrina, I'm glad to hear that you've had a good day. I've had a helluva day! Right now, you are so damn sexy, I think my day is going to get a lot better, so this is where I'd rather be."

Jake moved a little closer, and he could detect a quickening of her breathing as they both came together in a passionate embrace. Bathrobes dropped, their bodies touched. "Maybe we should go in." suggested Jake, his body quivering at the touch of her skin. They reached the bed, collapsing in a hot combination of soft caresses, gropes and burning kisses. The luxurious duvets softened the sounds of their moans of ecstasy and cries of passion.

# Vengeance - Chapter - 19

They both slept late the next morning, much to Matt's concern. As soon as Jake appeared, he attacked him with the news. "Good morning Jake . . . hope you slept well . . ." A knowing look on his face as he spotted Sabrina slowly coming down the stairs. "We have some answers back from Jacques. You're going to love this!"

"Can I get a cup of coffee first?" Jake asked, his mind still not clear.

"Oh yes, of course, I'm sorry." answered Matt. "Remember, we were trying to learn about this Ray Marko, the guy from X-Sells?"

"Of course I remember . . . what did Jacques tell you?"

"Well . . . this Ray Marko is actually Radomir Marković, a Serbian political hack. He's one of those fast talkers, con men, or whatever you call them. He was involved as campaign manager for several big name politicians in both Serbia and Bosnia. He was one of the gang that were going to be charged with war crimes, but they didn't have any direct evidence against him, and he just disappeared. Interpol usually keep their eyes on guys like that, so after the wars, they discovered he had moved to the U.S.A. He is fluent in English, so he was put in charge of X-Sells, which had just formed the year before. I assume our girl Dejana had something to do with that. Maybe they were either related, or they were bed-partners . . . it appears this gal has an unlimited supply of them."

Jake sipped his coffee, analyzing the data as he stared into space. Of course! It was obvious! The entire thing was run by the Serbian bitch! Her claws were very long and very sharp. She must have been setting this up for years . . . both in Europe and now in North and South America!

Sofia brought some large plates of breakfast and dropped them in front of Jake, derailing his train of thought. "Oh thank you Sofia," as he dug into the delicious food. Jake was starting to get used to the Argentine breakfast of *facturas,* a variety of pastries including *medialunes, bombas de fraille,* filled with *dulce de leche* or *crema pastelera.* Sabrina loved these sweet treats, but Jake's favourite was the savoury *Empanadas Catamarqueña.* It all went down well with either his coffee, or the highly caffeinated *yerba mate.*

Jake paused eating and turned to Matt "So what do we do with this information, especially as this guy is coming to town soon?"

"Well, I'm glad we know something about him before he arrived . . . but what we do with it . . . I have no idea. What do you think?"

"I think I'll ask Sabrina . . . she's got a good feel for things like this, and actually has more experience in law enforcement than I have."

"Well Jake, this isn't exactly law enforcement . . . otherwise I would know what to do."

With that they both started to laugh, then decided they would ask Sabrina, who at that moment was out on the patio with Elena, discussing girl things. The men called them in to ask their opinion on something, they glanced knowingly at each other, and agreed to come in.

Matt explained the situation and told them that this Ray Marko was coming to town. At first, the girls thought it humorous that the men had actually asked them for an opinion. Although both men normally didn't consult the girls on these things. Jake watched Sabrina as Matt explained the situation, and as he got to the point of mentioning Ray Marko's upcoming visit, he saw a distinct change on her demeanour.

"What is it Sabrina?" Jake asked quickly.

Sabrina was definitely disturbed, her brow wrinkled with concern. She knew they were all waiting for an explanation, so she started, shaking her head. "It's not just this guy . . . it's some history I've had with his type. The time I spent with our anti-terrorism group taught me a lot about some of these 'muscle-men' from the Balkans. It was these guys, from Bosnia, Serbia, Croatia . . . all over the former Yugoslavia . . . very tough, vicious, determined to succeed, and not concerned who gets in their way."

"OK, I think we know what kind of person we could be dealing with, but this isn't the Balkans . . . this is Buenos Aires . . . and we have a very effective police force here"

Sabrina started to laugh. "I'm sorry Matt," she said, "But you have no idea what these guys are capable of . . . how determined and vicious they can be. That 'little' encounter in Bregenz last summer was just a small example. The guy that the Serbian Bitch sent to get Landau was so determined, so dedicated to his cause, namely his lover, that he chose to die by poison before he was taken for questioning. He was also well trained . . . Spetsnaz trained, just like Landau. Training he needed in order to find and eliminate Landau." She stopped, thinking about her next words. "I think you should be thinking about why is he coming . . . what has changed . . . what is different now from a few weeks or a month ago?" She looked lovingly at Jake, then the others and added "I'd hate for you guys to come up against another monster like him. I don't want to lose you . . . either one of you!"

§

At the same time, Dejana Babić was working on yet another potion in her lab to add to her collection. Creating her potions was almost a treat for her, a way to relax. Her knowledge of botany and organic chemistry made things easy, and her natural ability to visualize the correct combinations helped her assemble some interesting potions. She loved working in her lab, especially when she had a problem she had to solve, or a business decision she had to make.

Her expansion into the South American market had started over two years before, when she realized the European scene was becoming too complicated with all of the countries and political interference. At first, she considered Brazil, with its massive impact on the Amazon forests and development of more farmlands. This eventually created a negative public opinion and back-lash against this work. An ideal situation for her business . . . those for and those against further development and it subsequent effects. Recent studies show that animal agriculture is contributing more to global warming than the petroleum industry. Brazil produced more than two hundred million livestock each year, more than the USA. The more she studied the situation, she realized the problem was huge, maybe too big to tackle first. So she decided to look at Argentina, where the cattle industry was about a quarter of Brazil's, at about fifty million. Knowing what little she did about Argentina, she was surprised that beef was the tenth largest food produced in Argentina, with soybeans being on top. This was a situation she could handle, she had 'experts' who could refute many of the claims about global warming and help the farming industry survive and prosper. With over five Billion dollars income from the beef industry at stake, she knew some of that could be hers.

While she worked, she kept thinking about Radović, and could almost feel herself becoming aroused as she remembered how he had excited her during their brief encounter earlier this year. It was when she decided to put him in charge of the California, indeed the entire USA operation. He was excited and very grateful, and he showed it in more ways than one. But now she was forced to use her 'ace-in-the-hole', play her trump card to achieve the results she needed. Her 'clients' demanded results, and with a huge amount of money at stake, she did not want to lose her share. Dejana decided she had to talk to Ray again, before he arrived in Buenos Aires.

# Vengeance - Chapter - 20

Radomir Marković was already getting used to his 'American' or anglicized name of Ray Marko. He had been in California running the operations of X-Sells for over a year now, and his success at his work had increased his status, both in the business sector and in the eyes of his employer Dejana Babić. He had discovered that his talking skills, his sales approach, had been his most effective weapon, managing to convince people of almost anything. He had surpassed Franco Martinez in successes mainly because he was more realistic, more ruthless in his approach, not so kind and gentle. He did not hesitate to use different techniques to convince a 'client' to move in a certain direction, so when Dejana asked him to go to Buenos Aires to 'check on things', he knew it meant to replace Franco if necessary, or do whatever other duties were necessary to achieve the desired result.

He arrived at the Buenos Aires Ezeiza airport totally unannounced. He purposely did not advise Franco of his flight information, as he wanted to 'be there' himself, and get a feel of the city, the country. Although more comfortable in either Serbian or English, Ray had a working knowledge of Spanish, which helped him immediately. He realized he was at a slight disadvantage, but he preferred to work at his own pace, according to his own agenda. What he had to accomplish would not require a fluency in Spanish.

He immediately hired a taxi to tour the city, he wanted to know where all of the environmental activist group leaders were staying. One by one, he checked them off his list, thinking each time that he had taken the first step in the process. Once that step was complete, he checked into a high end chain hotel in the centre of Buenos Aires. After a good meal and a few drinks, he relaxed and thought about his next move.

§

It wasn't until almost noon the next day when Franco heard from Ray. As the local rep for X-Sells, he was surprised that Ray had not advised him of his flight time, etc., so he could have picked him up, taken him to his hotel. After some brief comments, they agreed to meet at Ray's hotel to get to know each other and talk further.

"About my flight, etc., I didn't want to bother you." Ray said. "Besides, I prefer to make my own way. . . I learn more about the city that way."

"I can understand that." replied Franco, still a little puzzled at his boss's action. "Well . . . he started, what do you have in mind? Your email said you were coming to 'check things out'. What specifically did you want to 'check out'?"

Ray did not waste any time. "From what I know . . . there are almost a dozen environmental protesters in the city at this time. The whole idea of all of them meeting in Buenos Aires is to join forces . . . work together with a 'united front' . . . something they've never done before. What have you done to meet them, deal with them, evaluate their strengths, their techniques?"

"Whoa . . Ray . . . what are you talking about?" Franco said quickly.

"The only reason you are here is to stop, or at least slow down these groups. You can't do that unless you know what they are up to . . . how they are going to protest, how they are going to make their case. Then you can develop a plan to counter their moves." He stopped talking, looking at Franco. "You have a plan don't you? Just what are you doing here?"

Franco realized he was dealing with a different kind of person than he was used to. He immediately figured he'd better counter attack before this guy drove him into the ground. "Well, that episode with the cops last week sort of slowed things down."

"What episode with the cops? What are you talking about?"

Franco realized that this 'boss' wasn't as smart as he thought he was, and wasn't aware of the latest, so he'd better fill him in, but tread softly. "I don't know how much you know Ray, I thought you'd have been filled in a little before you came all this way 'to check things out'!" He couldn't help but drive home a few points of his own, before this guy started telling him he didn't know what was going on. "In case you don't know, a local politician, Tomas Romero, died . . . or I should say, was killed . . . murdered at one of our environmental rallies just over a week ago. He was my biggest opponent in the most recent argument, so of course, I was brought in by the police for questioning."

"Oh shit!"

"Yes, 'Oh shit!' . . . and of course, I didn't know anything, had nothing to do with it, but I have my suspicions, as do the police. These PFA guys are smart, and they even have a 'consultant' working with them on the case . . . some scientist from Canada."

"Double-shit! Is his name Prescott . . . Jake Prescott?"

"Yeah, I think that's him. I only met him once when I was brought in for questioning the second time."

"The second time? You've been questioned more than once?"

"Yeah, the first time we just talked about who might have dropped the poison into Romero's *mate,* but the second time we talked about X-Sell's parent company . . . some outfit in Serbia." He paused, noting the concerned look on Ray's face. "Do you know this Prescott?"

That bit of information hit Ray hard. "No . . . no . . . but I've heard of him." He had no idea that that local cops were that far ahead of him, or could add up those bits of information. He struggled to figure out a way to ask the next question. "How did they put that together? What lead them to that conclusions?"

"I don't know, but I think that 'consultant' Canadian scientist had something to do with it . . . apparently he's had a run-in with the company before, last summer in Bregenz."

"Yeah, I think I know who he is . . . like I said, I've heard about him." Ray had indeed heard about Jake Prescott, in fact the real reason he was here in Buenos Aires was to deal with Jake Prescott. He only knew part of the story about Bregenz, about Dejana's history with this guy, but he knew enough to consider the man as a worthy opponent, someone to be careful of, and now, someone to dispose of if possible. Dejana's hatred of Jake Prescott and his Interpol friend Jacques Manet ran deep. She had too many plans foiled, lost too many contracts and too much money because of those two meddling in her affairs. Although they were not directly involved, Dejana also blamed them for the death of her lover in that fiasco in Bregenz.

Ray backed off a little . . . as he figured he'd better learn more about Buenos Aires and the situation he had been sent to 'look over'. For sure, he'd better learn more about this Jake Prescott character before he went any further. He continued to probe Franco. "And the local cop . . . do you know him?"

The question surprised Franco. "Nooo . . .not really. I know he's good . . . I'm pretty sure he's in charge of the Romero murder. . . he was the one that questioned me when I was brought in . . . in the meeting with Prescott."

As soon as Franco left, Ray returned to his room . . . he knew he had to make a few calls.

§

With the five hour time difference between Beograd and Buenos Aires, Ray decided to wait until morning to call Dejana. From what he had learned from Franco, there was a lot more he'd better learn about this situation before he made any rash moves, and considering what Dejana had told him before he arrived in Buenos Aires, he knew he would have to make some of those moves. She hadn't given him any background details about her relationship with this Prescott, but he knew they were serious enough to be clouding her judgement.

# Vengeance - Chapter - 21

It was almost noon before Ray finally called Dejana in Serbia. He had been awake early that morning, but had been very busy making a few calls, both local and back to L.A.. He wanted to learn a few things about Prescott before he talked with Dejana, and when he finally made the call, he was glad he had prepared himself.

Lapsing into his native Serbian, Ray attacked Dejana as soon as she picked up the call. "What the hell is going on Dejana? You told me a little about this Prescott guy, but you failed to mention he was working with the police down here . . . apparently just like he did with Interpol in Bregenz. He's really tight with a local police guy, and has already pulled Franco in twice for questioning."

"Hold on Ray, I only told you what I knew . . . some of this has happened recently. I knew Franco was called in once, after that politician was found dead. When did the second one happen?"

Ray explained what he had learned from Franco, and they both agreed that Prescott and the police were a dangerous combination.

"Исус Христ! *Isus Hrist!* Jesus Christ!" Dejana's expletive exploded from the phone, confirming Ray's suspicion that this was not going well with his boss. "Once again . . . I have underestimated that son-of-a-bitch! He has caused me too much trouble . . . too much lost money . . . too much grief!" She paused thoughtfully, then added "That's it! I knew we should have done this when Kurt was around . . . I should have let him eliminate that damn Canadian last year! Do you know where he disappeared to? He's not at that hotel, we have to find out where he is." She stopped, staring blankly at Ray, her cheek muscles twitching as she began to form some words. "OK, that's it! We have to get rid of these obstacles as quickly as possible. This group of protesters will only be in town for another week, after that, we can't really do anything to earn our fee. I want that son-of-a-bitch dead!"

"O.K. Boss . . . I can do that!." Ray offered quickly, knowing he'd better find Prescott, fast!

§

Ray sat in his hotel room for over an hour longer, finishing the bottle of vodka he started yesterday. He rarely drank like this before lunch, but figured the circumstances called for some extra measures. The vodka relaxed him so he could just think and deal with the problem. A quiet room, no TV to disturb him, nothing else on his mind except the problem at hand. Where would a man like Prescott go? He has his girlfriend with him, and from what he was told, he has lots of money. So where?

The local cop! He was seen with him several times, and he is working for or with the PFA and Interpol again. There is must be an answer in that direction. He quickly pulled out the business card that Franco had given him, during his 'interview'.

He checked the information booklet in his room and found the number for the local police was the same as on the card. He didn't want to call the local 911 emergency number as he would be logged and traced if he tried to ask for any information. The local general information number for the PFA connected him to a polite young woman who was anxious to prove her worth.

"*Buenos Dias Señorita,*" Ray began. "I hope you can help me."

"*Por supuesto Señor!*" "Of course Señor, how can I help?"

"I have an important file for Officer Perez, but I haven't been able to find him for a couple of days. Do you know where he is?" He watched the girl hoping he didn't violate some internal protocol that would raise her guard.

"Oh, don't worry, just leave it here and I'll make sure he gets it."

Damn . . . not what I wanted, he thought. "No, that's OK . . . I've left it back in my hotel, maybe I'll just drop it off at his place."

"Well actually, you won't find him at his condo in town . . . he's taking a few days off and staying at his wife's parents at their B&B."

Great! Even better than he hoped. "That's why he's so hard to find" he laughed, "I'll give him a call there . . . what is the name of the B&B?"

The girl supplied the information with no hesitation, the entire episode an innocent inquiry. "It's the Santa Elena Estancia, out past San Antonio de Areco."

"*Muchas Gracias Señorita*".

"*De Nada!*"

§

Armed with that information, Ray now had to decide what to do with it. A B&B . . . a perfect place to invite an out-of-town guest to stay. No wonder he couldn't find them in town. He knew Prescott had his girlfriend with him . . . maybe he and the cop were old friends or something. He had learned that Prescott had arrived in Buenos Aires before the politician Romero was killed, so he must have been here just on vacation or maybe a visit to this local cop. Most likely didn't get involved with this matter until after he was here. That made more sense. Now, what to do?

The first thing Ray did was to look up the local tourist information on the *Santa Elena Estancia* B&B. He found a brochure in the hotel illustrating the estancia, run by Nicolas and Paula Sanchez, describing its features, facilities, location, etc. He was tempted to call them and book a few days for himself, but then realized that Perez and Prescott might know of him, or even know what he looks like. That would be very awkward, and raise too many complications. He worked on another plan. The hotel information desk had provided some details on some of the upcoming environmental events when he first arrived. Ray had planned his trip to include some time at these meetings and rallies that were sponsored by the local government and environmental groups from around the world. Tomas Romero had been killed during the first of these events, but several more even larger events were on the schedule, attracting Ray's eyes as he scanned the brochure.

§

At the same time, Jake Prescott was scanning the same brochure, thinking it might be a good idea to attend and learn about the situation in Argentina. He had become a little shy about attending these conferences as the last two he attended had resulted in murder and mayhem on a large scale. He had attended environmental events in Los Angeles and Vancouver, both of which had ended up with many people dead, including some friends and colleagues. This was a different type of conference, as it was more of a collection of environmental protest meetings, organized by several of the top environmental activist groups, but also sponsored by some government funding, a politically cautious move to make it look like they were concerned about global warming and climate change. As he talked to Matt about this possibility, he realized that the same characters were in play, who might repeat the same actions as in the past.

"In any case Matt, I think I'll take a couple of days and sign up for some of the events . . . I'm interested in a few of the papers that are being presented, and it's only on for another week." He stopped, then added "I think I'll ask Sabrina if she is interested . . . how about you and Elena?"

"I don't think so Jake, I lost interest in all that environmental stuff after I left you at university in Munich. Besides, I have a few other problems to work on now, remember?"

# Vengeance - Chapter - 22

It was a small meeting, only five of the groups involved. The candidate from Greenpeace spoke first. "Well gentlemen," he looked around, smiling, "I think you all agree that working with a united front was a good plan? First, I'd like to thank some of the local groups who made it possible for this united front by inviting us to their country. I won't mention all of the groups . . . mainly because I can't remember them all . . ." he laughed. "But I must mention the "Youth for Climate Action" organization who is working hard to get the young people involved in this crisis. And of course, the Extinction Rebellion, whose local chapter is growing fast, as is their world wide numbers. Despite the rather gloomy start to our efforts with the death of Tomas Romero, our numbers are making a significant statement here to the Argentine government and the leaders of the animal agriculture industry." He carried on with his speech . . . a speech he had not planned to make.

"I have a couple of extra points I wanted to make, and a few good bits of information you might be able to use. According to a recent paper that Greenpeace has published, animal protein provides only thirty-three percent of the world protein needs, yet takes seventy-seven percent of the world's agricultural land, and is the greatest driver of human caused deforestation."

He paused, pulling out a few more papers from his briefcase. "A lot of this stuff is common knowledge, at least to us, but it is always good to review some of these points, especially if you are heading into a debate. Most of these figures apply to the U.S.A. or global numbers, so you'll have to make adjustments or at least mention there might be a difference for Argentina."

Sorting the reports, he finally pulled one out and looked it over. "I know I'm probably boring you with a lot of numbers you've all heard many times before, but some of it bears repeating. This one is interesting . . . with respect to GHG emissions . . . Greenhouse Gas emissions. Measurements of methane, a very potent greenhouse gas, is about forty to ninety percent higher over animal farms . . . and methane can be from eighty to a hundred times more destructive than carbon dioxide." He scanned the group and added "Most of the people we will be dealing with will have some connections with the livestock industry . . . an industry that produces more than fifty-one percent of all worldwide greenhouse gas emissions." He flipped over another page . . . "Livestock is also responsible for sixty-five percent of all human related emissions of nitrous oxide, a greenhouse gas with almost three hundred times the global warming potential than carbon dioxide."

He paused again, obviously deep in thought and visibly disturbed by what he had just said. "I'm sorry, gentlemen . . . and ladies, these are just a few facts that disturb me greatly, and will no doubt disturb you as well. There are many more numbers like this in the papers I will be handing out. Ammunition for you to take to battle."

Some soft applause accompanied him as he took his seat, the others in the room equally affected.

§

Jake Prescott had just talked with his chemist, Alan Cook in Jake's office in Vancouver. Alan's words still rang in Jake's ears. "For God sake Jake, be careful down there . . . that whole animal agriculture versus the environment thing is dead serious. When I started researching things . . . especially this so-called environmental protest conference, or whatever they call it . . . it's just a powder keg ready to blow!"

"Oh come on Alan . . . aren't you exaggerating a little?" Jake asked.

"Well . . . OK, how about this? You know how important the Amazon rainforest is, and how much it's been in the news lately?"

"Yes, but what are you saying Alan?"

"You must know that animal agriculture is responsible for up to ninety-one percent of the Amazon destruction! More than one hundred thirty-six million rainforest acres are cleared for animal agriculture, and twenty-six million acres cleared for palm oil production."

"But . . ."

"No, let me finish. This is serious stuff! About one to two acres of the rainforest is cleared every second!"

"Holeee . . ."

"Yes, and that's not all. I found from my research that it is very dangerous to be an environmental activist down there. You're very familiar with the people we lost in Europe and North America in the past few years, and of course . . . this Tomas Romero in Argentina. . . the local politician that was killed. Well, welcome to the club! But down there . . .there have been something like *eleven hundred* land activists killed in Brazil in the past twenty years! . . . that's one thousand one hundred people Jake!'"

"Surely not . . . " Jake began.

"Yes Jake . . . this is very serious! And it's most likely similar in Argentina or any country involved in the deforestation for animal agriculture. It's been reported several times in respected journals, etc.. Even the New York Times had an article a few years ago by Rachel Nuwer called "The Rising Murder Count of Environmental Activists".

"Jesus, Alan . . . I had no idea . . . do you really think it's that bad?"

"Well, I was shocked as well Jake. I've checked several sources, had Peter run some extra internet searches. Those numbers are mainly related to Brazil, but I'm sure they apply to Argentina as well . . . they are into animal agriculture in a big way . . . and they are clearing the rainforest up north.

Jake shook his head, amazed at what Alan was telling him. He didn't know what to say. "Thanks Alan, I appreciate your research and your warning. I'll have to tell the rest of the gang here . . . maybe Matt knows more about this than what he's told me."

§

Jake found Matt and Elena out on the patio talking with Sabrina. "Perfect", he said as he joined them. "I think you have to listen to what Alan just told me." He repeated all of Alan's warnings and numbers and asked Matt if he knew anything about this. Matt and Elena exchanged glances, both looking a little guilty.

Well yes Jake, I did know some of those numbers . . . I haven't mentioned them because they are mainly newspaper sensationalism and besides, I didn't want to concern you with local politics, etc."

Elena interrupted with "Matt . . . don't be so obtuse! Tell them the truth . . they are all grown up people . . . they can take it."

"Yes . . . of course." answered Matt. "I'm little ashamed of our situation . . . but I guess it's happening all over the world." He paused to gather his thoughts and his next words. "There has been a definite upswing in environmental activism in recent times, and a lot of opposition to it . . . some of it quite violent, which affects my job considerably. There is another youth movement here called '*Jóvenes por el Clima Argentina*', Youth for Climate Argentina, involving students aged fifteen to twenty-nine from several provinces. I think they are trying to emulate the Thunberg movement in Europe. An organization called 'Extinction Rebellion', has grown lately, concerned with the '*Emergencia Climática y Ecológica*, the global warming problem that the United Nations experts are warning us about. "Yes, I'm familiar with those warnings, and the Extinction Rebellion . . . they are very big in the UK." Jake answered.

"Yes, well here in Argentina, more than twenty-five civil society organizations based across several provinces have joined forces to form a new climate alliance. I think they are involved in this protest consortium we are having now in Buenos Aires. Another outfit called Climate Save Argentina is trying to raise awareness over the impact of agriculture on the environment."

"So, basically yes," Matt said, "we have a big environmental concern here, and a growing interest and actions about it. The big statement for the day is '*Estamos en Emergencia Climática y Ecológica*'."

# Vengeance - Chapter - 23

Jake and Sabrina sat together on the patio, talking seriously with Elena's parents, Nicholas and Paula. Jake wanted to know more about the agriculture and environmental impacts of agriculture over the years. He had researched as much as he could online, but felt he needed a more personal input.

Argentina's agriculture industry was critical to the economy of the country. Ever since the Spanish *conquistadors* brought cattle to Argentina in the 1500's, they thrived on the endless *Pampas* grasslands. This grew into a thriving agricultural industry, prosperous farms, and massive herds of cattle. Over the years and centuries, the highly productive cattle industry played a major part in the culture of Argentina with the *gauchos*, or Argentine cowboys riding the pampas, and wealthy landowners of ranches or *estancias* building large houses, both on their farms as well as many of the major buildings in Buenos Aires. Their folklore also developed stories and legends around some of the gauchos, like the fabled *"Don Segundo Sombra"* from the famous novel by Argentine author *Ricardo Güiraldes*. Stories of their adventures on the pampas, their consumption of *mate*, a caffeine laced drink, and the ubiquitous *asado*, or barbecue of that plentiful beef, which eventually becomes the Argentine national dish. Other crops like soy, wheat, corn, sunflower, sorghum and rice use less than two percent of the farmland, but still play a major part in the country's economic prosperity.

"It was different in our day," Nicholas began, "The early settlers just went out and cleared some land, then planted crops to either harvest or to graze their cattle. The land was big . . . nobody ever thought there would come a day when they would run out of land, or their actions would eventually poison the earth." Nicholas was a kind man, and very intelligent, so he knew what the problems were. "And of course, several generations of this didn't make a great difference . . . until humans became very good at it! I'm saying they became very good at using the earth, actually destroying the earth. The machines became bigger, stronger, more efficient, so eventually, they were destroying land faster than it could heal . . . faster than it could recover."

He stopped a moment to take another mouthful of his wine . . . savouring it as he swallowed the ruby red potion. "And . . . to add to the problem . . . there are just too damn many people, too many people who enjoy a big Argentinian steak on the weekends . . . or even more often . . . so the demand becomes greater . . . to provide more steaks . . . we need more cattle . . . more land . . . more of everything!"

Everyone was quiet . . . absorbing what Nicholas was telling them. He continued in a quiet voice. "Yes Jake and Sabrina . . . we have a real problem here . . . a dangerous problem, both for the immediate and distant future." He paused a moment, recalling another point. "Not only that, if things get out of control, you'll have to deal with the hungry and sometimes violent section of our society."

"What do you mean 'hungry and violent'?"

"Back in the seventies and eighties, during a particularly rough time, there were people who used to wander the countryside, the pampas, killing our cattle, just to survive! When the economy is stressed, so are the people and they will do anything to survive." He stopped again, looking over to

Claudia and then Elena. "Elena was telling us you had some fun on our shooting range while we were away. We used to do that a lot . . . not only for our hunting excursions, but for basic self protection. That's why we still have a lot of guns and ammunition in the house . . . just in case? We just can't continue down this path of destruction and consumption and not expect some unexpected and undesirable consequences."

Jake thought about that and added "So, I see now why all these environmental activists have descended on Buenos Aires, and why they are working together . . . it's too important to leave it up to individual organizations."

"That's about it!"

§

Ray knew about Danko, what he managed to achieve, and how he had rendered himself useless by becoming known to the police. After arranging with Dejana to contact Danko, they decided to meet in a quiet bar close to where he lived. Ray understood Danko, the way he thought, the way he operated. He had worked with many like him over the years . . . people he could trust to do a job, after all, he was one of them.

They were almost through the bottle of vodka when they decided on a plan. Both of them knew that their boss, Dejana was totally pissed off with this Canadian Jake Prescott, and the Interpol guy Jacques Manet. There was not much they could do about Manet, and Dejana told them she would handle him as well, just to make it complete.

They both poured over the meetings scheduled during the next week. More importantly, they were studying where each of the rallies were held, especially group protest meetings when multiple organizations were planning on being there.

Danko pointed to one of the information sheets. "See that one . . . I know that meeting hall . . they have big parties and

Tango dance-offs there. I guess they've rented it for these groups."

"So . . . is there something that will help us with that knowledge?"

Yeah . . . I know the guy that manages the place . . . we could have access to the whole building . . . I just have to grease a few palms . . . one in particular."

"Great! So what do you have in mind?"

"I'm not sure just yet, but it is not going to be good for everyone inside that building. We just have to make sure Mr. Prescott is at that meeting."

Ray had an idea what Danko was planning.

"So what are you thinking Danko . . . assuming we can get Prescott in that room?"

"The room is supplied with very efficient air conditioning because of the active dance events that are held all during the year." "So . . . " Danko continued, thinking as he spoke . . . "What would happen if the air conditioning failed, or started pumping in something other than cool air?"

Ray nodded, realizing Danko might have something here, a way to kill two birds with one stone, so-to-speak, maybe even more that two birds. He watched Danko closely as he realized the man was very much like others he had dealt with over the years, very capable and very dangerous.

"O.K., you work on that Danko, let me know if you come up with a viable plan, and let me know if you need some help or even more money to get the job done!"

§

Danko called his friend Jose as soon as he finished with Ray and arranged to meet him for drinks.. He had met Jose Dominique shortly after he had arrived in Buenos Aires. Jose was a mechanical wizard, and was responsible for the maintenance of the same night club Danko worked at as well as the one that was going to be used for the environmental rallies.

"So, tell me Jose." Danko started, "Do you ever have problems with the air circulation in those buildings?"

Jose was a little surprised at the question, studying Danko's face closely. "We have had some problems . . . why do you ask?"

Danko knew he had to be very careful with the next question. "No, I was just wondering . . . they really need good air circulation, or fresh air makeup with all the smoking, fancy dancing and other activities."

"Yeah, that's always a problem . . . both in summer and winter."

"Why in winter?" Danko asked, "Can't you just open the doors more, at least you shouldn't need the air conditioning?"

"No, no air conditioning, but in the winter we have to fire up the furnace . . . it can get pretty cold."

Danko almost jumped. The furnace . . . of course . . . why didn't he think of that. "Are the furnaces ever used in the summer, like now?" he asked.

"Only if we have a cold spell." Jose answered. "Very rarely. In fact we're having the one in that other building serviced right now . . . had some problems with it last winter. All our furnaces and air conditioners are being retrofitted from use of oil to gas . . . burns a lot cleaner"

"What kind of problems?'

All the furnaces have to be serviced periodically, make sure they burn efficiently, don't produce carbon monoxide or have it leak into the system.

With that last statement, Danko knew he had found the answer to his problem. He had used carbon monoxide in the past as a weapon, and it looked like he might use it again. He smiled at Jose and ordered another round of drinks.

# Vengeance - Chapter - 24

Jake and Sabrina were getting ready to head into town when Matt knocked on their door. "Hey guys . . . you ready yet? I'd like to get there early . . . the parking around that place is terrible."

"So, do we need tickets? Where do we buy them?"

"No problem . . . that Ray Marko dropped off some tickets at the office for us, compliments of X-Sells."

Don't you guys have rules against that . . . accepting gifts from firms?

"Yes, but this doesn't count, the tickets are free, they only limit them because the venue is quite small . . . and besides, it's an environmental rally, they want as many people as possible to come and listen."

§

Before long, they were parked and heading into the meeting hall. Colourful banners and posters decorated the hall, illustrating the normal use of the place. Life-sized, cardboard cutouts of sexy tango dancers and singers were strategically placed around the entrance and along the insides of the hall. At one end of the room, there was a fully equipped bar off to one side, and a small stage in the centre, decorated with banners and environmental messages sponsored by several of the activist organizations. On the stage, several chairs were placed in a semi-circle around the podium and microphone.

Matt and Elena led the way, finding some seats for the four of them along one side of the hall. "Come on guys, we can see everything from here, and are close enough to heckle the speakers". Matt was laughing as he poked Jake in the side.

"For sure Matt." Jake answered. "Actually, I'm really interested in listening to these guys . . . even with all the environmental events I have attended over the years, this is probably the first actual protest rally I have been to."

They were all laughing as they took their seats and waited for the events to begin. They looked around, soaking up the Buenos Aires ambience of the room.

They didn't have to wait long before several of the speakers arrived and took their seats on the stage. Jake recognized a couple of them, mainly from media exposure over the years, newspaper articles, TV news reports, and industry publicity. He also recognized Franco Martinez, the X-Sells man that he and Matt had interviewed at the police office. He was sitting up close to the stage, ready to join the discussion if necessary. He began to feel excited to be here, as he felt many of the speeches he would hear today would be very important and relevant to his work. He hoped the speeches would be available in printed form so he could pass them on to his crew in Vancouver.

"Boy, it's going to get pretty hot in here." Matt said as they closed the doors to any further visitors. "I just hope the air conditioning works well."

The master of ceremonies opened the meeting with a brief welcome speech to all of the organizations present, with a special welcome to several of the government officials and a couple of representatives from the cattle industry. "We sincerely hope that this kind of meeting of the minds can further our knowledge and understanding of the severe problems we are facing now, with some ideas of possible solutions."

Those words began a preamble that set the tone for the meeting, each of the organizations took turns to make their case against the animal agriculture industry. Jake could see some of the candidates cringe as many of the facts and figures were quoted.

Not long into the meeting, a spokesperson for the cattle industry asked to be heard. She was a very tall, well tanned lady, who had probably spent most of her life riding a horse and dealing with the cattle first hand.

Jake looked up her name on the information pamphlet they had received on arrival. She was a well known estancia owner with at least two degrees in agriculture and animal husbandry.

"Well," thought Jake, "This should be interesting."

The woman stood at the podium and took command of the room. "From what I am hearing today . . . you're basically trying to tell us to shut down our ranches, close up our estancias, and dispose of all our cattle? All this because somebody in some foreign country figures it's not good for the environment? We've been doing this for hundreds of years, many generations of families living off the raising of cattle. It's what we do in Argentina . . . and many other countries I might add!"

"Well, no." another speaker interrupted her. "We're just pointing out the damage that animal agriculture is doing. Studies show that it is contributing more than eighty percent of the greenhouse gases. Until now, everyone was blaming the petroleum industry, automobiles, trucks, the entire transportation industry as the major offender. We now see that animal agriculture is a big player . . . and not just greenhouse gas, but the use . . . I'd venture to say waste . . . of natural resources."

"So . . . what are you suggesting? Do you have some magic solution to this . . . something we can live with?"

Jake could feel the argument heating up . . . in fact the entire room seemed to be heating up. He turned to the others and whispered "Is anybody else feeling the heat? I hope the air conditioning is OK, it doesn't seem to be working very well." They all nodded in agreement, but nothing was said.

The activist speaker continued to respond to the 'cattle lady'. "Unfortunately madam, the numbers not only show the emissions caused by your industry, but we also have to consider the massive destruction of forest areas to provide you with more land for your animals, and to grow more food for your animals. Again, the statistics are against you. More than eighty percent of farmland is used for livestock, but only produces about eighteen percent of the food calories. Water use is almost criminal, as we are facing a world-wide shortage of water in the foreseeable future. For equivalent food value or calorie content, the beef industry consumes almost fifty times the amount of water than plants!"

Some of the speakers on the stage were feeling the heat, and had called the caretaker of the building. Jake looked over to his group and could see they were not faring well. He started to feel a little dizzy, and the stage was beginning to appear blurry. As he looked over the crowd, he saw two older participants who appeared in distress, then he watched in horror as they keeled over in a faint, crashing against others who were seated.

He looked across and could barely see Matt yelling at him. "Jake . . . something's wrong . . . can you get over to that emergency door? We need to get some air in here, *muy pronto!*"

All four of them stood up and tried to move towards the door, which seemed very close, but very difficult to reach. Jake rose to his feet, stumbled over a couple of fold-up chairs, almost fell. He struggled towards the door, it seemed so far away . . . finally got there and hit the emergency door release as he staggered outside. As the door opened, an alarm went off in the building. He gasped great lung fulls of air that was much fresher and slightly cooler than the inside air. He turned and helped Sabrina and Elena outside. Many participants had collapsed . . . others obviously in trouble. A few were starting to move towards the exit door. They were very quiet, slowly shuffling along, trying to support others as they moved towards the fresh air. Before long, Matt had cleared his head and was calling an emergency number on his phone as he helped other patrons to leave the room.

Within minutes, they heard the sirens of emergency vehicles arriving. The first thing the firemen did was check around the room and open up other doors, allowing the air to move through. They then walked through all the seated area and found a few more victims, passed out from whatever had affected them. The emergency medical techs were administering oxygen, working on as many as they could handle, eventually calling for an extra ambulance and crew to help transport the worse case victims to the hospital.

Once they had been thoroughly checked over and released by the medical people, the four of them decided to go for a coffee and recover a little. Matt told the group "The med-techs have suggested we stay quiet and rest for a while . . . make sure there are no further symptoms or side effects. The fire department's hazmat team are taking samples now, trying to figure out what that was."

"From what I saw" offered Jake, I would guess carbon monoxide . . . I've got a terrible headache . . . and still having trouble clearing my vision."

# Vengeance - Chapter - 25

All four of them felt they had a severe hangover for the rest of the day. After the doctors had checked each one of them, they were released, but told to watch out for additional symptoms. Several victims were still in the hospital, people who already had compromised respiratory systems. The oxygen is helping, but some were still in critical condition. From what Matt had learned, the cause of their problems was carbon monoxide from a malfunctioning heating system. They were given a lecture on the dangers of carbon monoxide, a colourless, odourless, deadly-poison gas. If they had been trapped in that room just a short time more, they would have lost consciousness and died within minutes. The doctor told them that in the USA, more than four hundred people die each year from CO, but over twenty thousand people are admitted to the hospital from CO exposure.

"Heating system? Why was the heating system on? asked the girls. "It was a hot day . . . we needed AC, not heat."

"Apparently it was being serviced, they do that sometimes during the nice weather. Something went wrong and there was some kind of leak in the exhaust system." Matt answered.

Jake was in deep thought throughout the discussion, "I don't know folks . . . it all sounds too fishy to me . . . just a little too convenient. Maybe I'm just getting paranoid, but I honestly think that whole episode was aimed at us."

"Us?" Elena choked out. "Whatever gives you that idea... who would do such a thing?"

Sabrina answered immediately. "You know who..." she said. "Our lady in Serbia! With all her connections here, I wouldn't doubt she has a standing order to dispose of us... or at least some of us... and most likely worth a lot of money, I'd guess." She looked at Jake with a furrowed brow. "What do you say Jake?"

"My thoughts exactly, my love. I've got to check with Jacques in Lyon... better still, Matt, can you do that, he's your boss... find out what kind of communications traffic there has been lately. I think I'll call Peter in my office to find out the same thing."

"*Jesús Cristo!*" yelled Matt. "Who would put dozens of people at risk to just dispose of one or two people?"

Sabrina answered quickly again. "That's what I've been trying to tell you guys! This group does not hold back, just because somebody gets in the way. It's just racked up as collateral damage... the cost of doing business."

With those facts and speculations in mind, the entire scene took on a different atmosphere. It appeared that they, or some of the group were being hunted, seriously hunted.

§

Mateo Perez was definitely worried. This entire event had taken them all by surprise. He remembered Sabrina's warning words and her serious concern for their safety. It was obvious that she had seen more of this kind of behaviour than he had. He blamed himself for being so naive, not considering that such an event could be planned and executed with such ruthlessness. Because of the nature of the accident and the number of victims involved, the PFA had opened a serious investigation into the incident. In addition to his work with Interpol's NCB office in

Buenos Aires, Matt worked closely with the local Argentinian investigators to track down what had happened. As most of the people involved were from other countries, they took particular care and attention to the investigation. Matt kept abreast of the proceedings, reporting to Jacques Manet at Interpol Headquarters with every new finding or detail, and also keeping Jake and the others 'in the loop'.

Jacques Manet was particularly worried. Similar to Jake, he had seen things like this before and knew how dangerous it could be to ignore the signs. He was privately glad that Sabrina, his favourite heroine, was on site to analyze the data. Although he was worried about her security and safety, he knew she had the experience and first hand knowledge to recognize the M.O. (method of operation) of these criminals, and knew how far they would go to achieve their goals. He stared out his office window, looking down on the Rhone River and surrounding countryside. He thought about Jake Prescott, shaking his head. "My God, he's done it again!" he said to nobody in particular. "How does he do it . . . how do these things follow Jake around . . . or does he just promote them?'

He turned to his intercom. "Annette, could you please get me Jake Prescott's office? I want to talk to Peter Wong. . . and to Alan Cook while I'm at it." He glanced at his watch. "If they are not open, leave a message for somebody to call me first thing in the morning."

§

Dejana Babić was also worried. Ray and Danko's pathetic attempt to dispose of Prescott did not work. It was close, but did not achieve their goal. The result was even worse . . . an attack like that on an international group was bound to raise alarms. She could only hope that the investigation did not reveal much . . . but she knew that if Prescott and Manet at Interpol were involved, they would not be satisfied until they had some good answers. Why did Danko try to use carbon monoxide? It was so sloppy and unreliable . . . there were too many variables, too many ways it could fail. In addition, when multiple deaths are involved, it draws too much attention to the event. One person killed in a heating system accident was understandable, almost accepted, but several people dead creates a lot of unanswered questions. Even worse, if there are dozens of deaths, they do whatever is necessary to find those responsible and all Hell is brought down on whoever is involved. She thought to herself "I guess that's why I like poisons . . . once I set things in motion, there is no turning back." Dejana wondered if this was a good time to work on the Manet problem, but decided against it as there would be heightened security around him for sure.

Now in Buenos Aires she had to deal with not only extra security, but an active investigation by both Interpol and the Argentine PFA. She would have to tread lightly and tell her men to back off a little and 'lay low'.

§

Once Ray and Danko received their orders, both of them were glad to 'lay low'. The extra police interest had spooked them both, making any further action too risky. They knew that any additional activity in their banking or large cash transactions were subject to close scrutiny and were avoided. Danko was glad he had enough cash available to continue without making any large withdrawals that could trigger police interest.

For the week following the disastrous meeting, nothing happened. Most of the participants had returned to their own countries or places of business and things returned almost to normal.

In contrast, the police were very busy, both the PFA and Interpol, trying to tie it all together, yet frustrated by their lack of legal evidence to work with.

Ray felt OK about 'laying low' for a short time, but knew he wanted to achieve his goal . . . that is, eliminate Jake Prescott and policeman friend, and he was thinking about a way he could do it, but he needed Dejana's help to set it up.

## Vengeance - Chapter - 26

A couple of days later, Jacques Manet called Matt to discuss the 'case'. Jacques knew that Jake would be involved and secretly hoped that Sabrina would also be listening. As it happened, there were four people in Argentina and one in France on a conference call to discuss the latest developments.

"Jolly good!" Jacque's voice boomed out of the speakerphone. "I'm so glad you could all make it to my party!" He paused, then started with "Mateo, my boy . . . I'll let you begin with your latest findings on our friend Danko Dragonović."

"Thanks Jacques. Since the 'event', we have been doubling our efforts to find this Danko character. He was picked up a couple of days ago, says he just took a few days off, nothing incriminating that we can hang on him."

A collective groan went through the group, as they were convinced that he had something to do with all of this.

"But . . . " continued Matt. "We learned that the same guy who services the air-con heating system at the meeting hall also does the same service at the nightclub where Danko works."

You could almost hear a collective 'Aha!' from the others.

"So that gave us some common links to work on. This guy has been brought in for questioning and we are hoping to establish further connections. In the meantime, we are monitoring Danko's calls, and also Ray Marko's calls . . . I still don't trust him."

"I wouldn't trust either of them." added Jake. "I have to agree with Sabrina . . . these guys are serious, and are very smart at what they do."

Matt did not agree totally. "If he was that smart, we wouldn't be here, or tracking down clues. There appears to be a connection, but we need legal proof before we can do anything."

"I realize you guys are restricted to following the rules, but I am not bound by those rules."

"Come on Jake . . . you know you can't do anything stupid!" Matt said.

"No, nothing stupid, in fact very smart. I'm going to have Alan and Peter track these guys, trace and record every call, and find out just what they are up to. I know, it might not be allowed in a court case, but it will give us a 'heads up' in case any more missiles are coming our way."

Jacques interrupted at this point with "Right-O Jake! I agree! We have to start thinking like these blokes. Interpol is getting warrants to tap the Serbian bitch's phone. Unfortunately, each time we try it, she is one step ahead of us and changes her tactics, or changes phones, so we get nothing! This woman is very, very clever! I sometimes wish she was working for us."

At that moment, Matt's work phone rang. He answered and was quickly involved in a discussion with his main investigators on the case. He looked pleased when he finally hung up. "Well folks, we're making a little progress. That serviceman who works at the nightclub and the meeting hall just deposited a large amount into his bank account . . . several thousand dollars. Unfortunately, is was a cash deposit so we probably have no chance finding out where or who it came from."

Jake asked "Matt . . . what have these guys been up to in the last week? You haven't mentioned anything and the conference/ protest thing is over, everyone has gone home."

Matt answered with a sour look on his face. "Unfortunately, they haven't been up to anything! I think that after that fiasco at the meeting hall, they got orders to back off and go to ground."

Jacques interrupted with "I agree. There has been little or no communication between them and their 'head office'. I think our 'Poison Pal' in Serbia is pissed off with these guys. You know how much she likes poisons . . . very specific . . . none of this mass murder stuff . . . tends to attract too much attention."

Jake looked over to Sabrina and asked "What do you think Sabrina. Does this sound right?"

"Yes, I have to agree, but keep your guard up. They just might be planning another offensive, but this time even deadlier because they are all getting pissed off and impatient." She paused a moment then added "In fact this hiatus really scares me, because we have no idea what they will try to do next!"

They all looked at Jake, waiting for his input. His mind was in a turmoil, processing the data and trying to figure out what they were up to. The only thing he could come up with so far was the obvious sequence of their actions and the obvious motivations that they were familiar with.

"Well . . . I think that what started as a plan by our gal in Beograd has turned into a vendetta against me. Her business, as far as we know, is a 'murder for hire' type thing where large companies hire her to dispose of or deter certain people from doing things that are bad for the bottom line . . . cut into their profits. We've seen this in Europe . . . she was tracking down and disposing of leading scientists who were trying to warn against global warming." He stopped, then looked over to Matt. "Remember Matt . . . this all started when that politician was killed at that environmental rally . . . he was talking about the dangerous effects of animal agriculture . . . something you can't do in Argentina and get away with it. I think she was hired to 'muzzle' these voices and slow down this big joint environmental protest meeting started."

"But,"

"No . . . let me finish. Enter . . . Jake Prescott! Actually, Jake Prescott and his gang of crime fighters!" This brought laughs from all of them, but then serious looks as they realized what Jake was saying. "We arrived on the scene quite by accident. Sabrina and I just wanted some 'down time', and again by accident met up with an old friend Mateo. To make things worse, or better, depending on how you look at it, Matt works not only for the Interpol NCB, right here in Buenos Aires, but also with the Argentine PFA. Once we began talking together, certain questions were asked, certain answers resulted, and the whole thing became another puzzle for us to solve. I think that our girl in Beograd saw this and realized what was going on . . . another frustrating move by that pesky Canadian scientist/ amateur detective. I firmly believe that this is what changed her direction . . . she realizes she has to get rid of me, and maybe anyone who works with me so she can get her business back to normal."

They all stared at Jake as his words slowly sank in. Jacques was the first to respond. "Right-on again Jake! I think you are correct in your analysis. From what we have seen here . . . she has included me in that mix as well. I know she has a contract out to dispose of me as soon as convenient."

The next few minutes included a lot of soul searching and thoughts of self preservation as they tried to take in what they had just been told.

Matt stood up and announced "Thank you Jacques . . . I think that's it for this meeting . . . we'll get back to you. Right now we have to have another meeting to decide what our next move is."

# Vengeance - Chapter - 27

Franco Martinez was not as lucky. He woke up three days later in the hospital with what he called the *'madre de todos los dolores de cabeza''*, or 'the mother of all headaches'. From what he learned from the nurses and his doctor, he was fortunate to be alive. A few more minutes in that room and his brain damage would have been too severe. Because he was close to the stage, at floor level, he was one of the last to reach fresh air, not under his own power, but with a fireman dragging him, administering oxygen soon after. Franco didn't remember much before things went black. just that it was hot and stuffy.

The nurses were very cooperative, very glad to be talking to this handsome Spaniard, and anxious to make him as comfortable as possible. When Franco started asking questions about what had happened, they were only too glad to find out whatever details they could. Before long, even from his hospital bed, Franco had pieced together a pretty good picture about the entire scene. What he learned disturbed him. He began to doubt whether his company was as innocent as they tried to depict. He knew what Ray and that other fellow Danko were capable of, and it bothered him to be associated with such activities. He asked more questions about the episode . . . if anyone had died. He learned nobody had died, but two people were in critical condition and still in a coma. The nurses brought him some newspapers which filled in much of the detail. The rally had finished shortly after the event and most of the attendees had returned home to their normal place of work.

His next problem was "what was he going to do about it?" The first thing . . . get out of this hospital. "No", his nurses said, "you have to rest at least one more day while we do more tests. We still don't know how much damage was done to your brain."

Franco had to agree, his brain really did feel like it had been fried. "OK, maybe a short nap" he managed to say before he passed out.

Four hours later, he woke up, feeling much better and determined to get out of the hospital. He knew one of the first things he wanted to do was to contact that police guy and the Canadian guy that had interviewed him.

§

By the time the taxi dropped him off at his apartment, Franco was exhausted. He didn't realize just how much of a toll the experience had taken on his body. As he closed the door behind him, all he wanted to do was collapse in his chair and have a drink. He had second thoughts . . . maybe a drink wasn't a good idea, considering the frail condition of his brain. "Boy!" he said to himself, "I can't believe this . . . how much were those other poor *desafortunados,* suffering?" Before he allowed his body to surrender to sleep again, he pulled out his phone and punched out the numbers from Mateo's card.

"Mateo Perez, please." he asked when the phone connected. He waited, listening to the response. "Could you please have him call Franco Martinez as soon as possible? He has my number . . . yes . . . it's about the meeting hall accident . . . the one where everyone was gassed!" The person on the phone told him that Mateo would call him back in a few minutes.

Franco hung up and waited . . . not sure he was doing the right thing. "Of course you are doing the right thing." he told himself.

It was only a minute later when his phone rang. Mateo Perez was indeed interested in what Franco had to say. "Can we meet somewhere to talk?" Franco asked.

"Of course . . . do you have somewhere in mind?"

"How about right here in my place?" Franco asked. "I can even put on some coffee, or do you prefer *mate*?"

Mateo showed up twenty minutes later and they both sucked on some *mate* as Franco wondered how he was going to start this. Mateo asked "How are you feeling . . . you were out of it for a couple of days?"

"I'm fine now, but it was close. There are a few others not so lucky." Franco answered, then asked "I understand you were there . . . how are you?"

"We're fine."

"We?"

"Oh, I hadn't mentioned. Remember the Canadian guy you met in my office?"

"Yeah . . . the tall guy with the cane?"

"Yes, that's him. Jake Prescott is a scientist who specializes in environmental matters. He, his girlfriend, myself and my wife were there to listen to the speeches, and we all just narrowly escaped."

"O.K. . . . " Franco paused. "That explains a few things."

"What do you mean, explains a few things?"

Matt watched the man . . . something was bothering him which he was having trouble explaining. "Why don't you just tell me what's on your mind Franco . . . I can see something is stuck in your head."

He started right off with "I think my company is responsible for that attack!" He knew right away that once he 'let the cat out of the bag', he would have to explain it, and doing so would release a lot of pressure on that mother of all headaches he was still trying to ease.

"O.K.," started Matt, "That's a pretty bold and incriminating statement Franco . . . would you care to expand?"

Matt was momentarily at a loss. He wished Jake was there as he knew somebody else should be in the room to listen. "Go ahead" he asked. "I might have you repeat or explain things as we go . . . I don't think either of our minds are working at full capacity."

"For sure!" agreed Franco. "When I woke up, I had the worst headache of my life . . . and it is not much better a few days later." He shifted his position in his chair and continued. "When we talked last, I mentioned my suspicions about the parent company in Serbia that might be controlling all this. I think they are still controlling and directing some of these 'accidents' that are happening to the key environmental people or anyone raising trouble for the animal agriculture folks. I emphasize 'animal agriculture' rather than just say cattle raisers or cattlemen . . . it's related to all animal agriculture that's causing the main problem."

"So . . . Franco . . . what are you saying?"

"That other Serbian, Danko is his name . . . I think he was responsible for causing the furnace to malfunction and release CO into the room."

"You think? Or do you know? Can you prove any of this?"

"Well . . . not really . . . but I think he and my boss Ray have been planning something."

"What do you mean . . . planning something?"

"They had a meeting a few days ago . . . Danko works at that nightclub in San Telmo . That's where he knows the maintenance guy . . . the same maintenance guy that works at the meeting hall where the rally was."

"Yes Franco, we already know that fact. What we don't know is if Danko or Ray actually asked or paid this guy to do something. Have you seen or heard of any meetings before . . . or since as a matter of fact.?"

Franco suddenly appeared to be in deep thought. Matt was convinced he just remembered something important.

# Vengeance - Chapter - 28

Matt called Jake as soon as he left Franco's.apartment. "Jake . . . I think we have something. I just had a little session with our friend Franco Martinez. He was just released from the hospital and I think his close call had quite an effect on him. He's a little pissed off with some of the others in that X-Sells outfit."

They met at Matt's office at the PFA. Jake had arrived shortly after Matt had returned from his meeting with Martinez. It was the first time Jake had been in Matt's office, and was fascinated by the photos, papers, notices and clues posted on the white board behind his desk. "I'm glad you like it Jake . . . this is pretty well everything we know about the case. I'm hoping that the information that Franco Martinez can provide might help tie this up."

"Franco was in the hospital for a couple of days wasn't he?"

"Yeah, almost finished him. I think there are still two more in a coma from that event."

"I've seen some of the damage caused by CO before. It is a very insidious gas . . . colourless, odourless, tasteless. Not only is it normally undetectable to a person, it works in your system, combining with the haemoglobin in your blood, basically making it ineffective. If it continues for any time period, and you don't get some real oxygen, that's when you get these brutal headaches, nausea, and sometimes into a coma . . . like those two still in the hospital."

§

Dr. Dejana Babić was deep in thought after her call from Ray in Buenos Aires. Ray knew she had connections with a few Serbian gang members, and was asking for some help. Dejana did know a few people 'in the business', but had made sure she stayed clear of that type for most of her career. She found that that drug trade and associated dealings tended to attract too much attention, too much interest by the police, especially if it is an international effort.

Every since the European Police Office (EUROPOL) had released its report on drug trafficking from South America through the Balkans and the Black Sea in Eastern Europe, Dejana had been very wary about getting associated with anyone in that group. In recent years, together with Interpol and local law enforcement, over fourteen people had been arrested in an investigation called "Warrior of the Balkans", involving five major organized crime gangs in Serbia, mainly the *Zemun clan,* led by Željko Vujanović. The most recent was a Buenos Aires resident, Carlos Gallego, in the Palermo district, along with others involved in the Serbian/Argentine/Europe cocaine drug transport and distribution.

She knew many of the those involved were still around, some still active in the business. What she needed at this point was some dependable contacts in Buenos Aires, people she could hire to accomplish a few jobs. Dejana had given it a lot of thought, and had finally decided she had to change her methods, and 'get serious' if she ever wanted to get rid of that Canadian scientist and determined Interpol agent in Lyon. A few telephone calls later, she had some contacts in Buenos Aires who were guaranteed to do the job.

§

Dejana knew that her girl in Interpol was hesitant to follow her orders and deal with her boss, Jacques Manet. For over a year now, the extra money given to Malina's aunt in Beograd had enticed her enough to supply 'inside' information on what was happening. The information on the whereabouts of Jake Prescott and some of the communications between Prescott and Manet had been very valuable. Now Dejana wanted to end the entire game. Prescott had caused enough trouble by himself, and in concert with Manet, had been a disaster for her business.

She felt she had a handle on the Buenos Aires situation, both with Ray Marković on site, and some other characters in motion, and knew she had to make a serious move herself to eliminate Jacques Manet from the scene. The only problem . . . Dejana was suspicious Malina was not up to the job. All she had to do was drop a little of her special potion into his coffee one day, but Malina knew what the result would be and refused to do it. Dejana had to take more aggressive action. She called Malina at home one evening on her private line.

"Malina . . . first I would like to thank you for being such a help. I'm sure your aunt has enjoyed the extra money she has received for the past year, but now I must ask you to take the next step. I can't afford to have Jacques Manet interfere with my business any more, and I'm sure you wouldn't want anything to happen to your aunt would you?"

Dejana did not pull any punches, she wanted her objectives to be very clear. She tied both subjects together so Malina would understand what is at stake . . . what she must do.

"What . . . what are you saying? Are you actually saying that something might happen to my aunt if I don't do what you want?"

"Well . . . I know it doesn't sound good when you say it like that Malina, but yes . . . I have reached my limit."

Malina carefully acted horrified at the suggestion, but she was not really surprised. She knew that one day Dejana would ask her just that. She struggled to appear upset at the prospect of killing her boss. She already had an answer for Dejana . . . a way to stall things for some time and allow her to put her own plan into action.

"I must think about this Dejana for a couple of reasons. First, we talked about this last month . . . I don't have any more of that potion you gave me. Remember? I threw it out during the mixup with Landau last year." She stopped . . . not expecting an answer, but then continued before Dejana had time to reply. "I'm going back again to visit my aunt in about two weeks . . . maybe we can meet and I can get some more."

Dejana digested this information and thought it could be a reasonable solution to her problem. She checked her calendar and marked down a few notes. "Yes . . . OK, sounds good. Just keep that in mind . . . I am very close to where your aunt lives, so don't forget. I wouldn't want to see her hurt in any way."

§

Jake and Sabrina were enjoying an evening with Elena's family at the estancia when one of the estancia's gauchos cautiously approached the patio. "*Perdóneme Jefe,* Pardon me Boss, but I'd like to tell you something."

"Of course Marco . . . please . . . come and sit down." Pointing to Jake and Sabrina he asked "Have you met our guests . . . Señor Prescott and Señorita Wagner?"

"No *Patrón,* I have heard their names from Sofia only." He turned to Jake and Sabrina *"Encantado de concerte*, pleased to meet you. Welcome to *Estancia Santa Elena!"*

"Now Marco . . . what is it you want to say to me. Our guests might be interested as well, while they are enjoying their stay at our *estancia.*"

"I might be getting a little too suspicious Jefe, but there have been two hunters wandering the far pastures for two days . . . sometimes coming close to the house."

"The hunters come quite often to shoot doves. Why do you wonder?"

"They don't look like hunters. And they do not have *la escopeta*. shotguns, but very high power rifles with *miras telescópicas,* telescopic sights."

"That is unusual" agreed Nicholas. "Maybe you could ask the men to keep track of these 'hunters' . . . and we'll see what they are up to."

"*Si Patrón.*"

# Vengeance - Chapter - 29

After Marco had returned to his duties, Nicholas turned to his guests and said "I'm sorry folks, I think maybe Marco is a little too suspicious and protective these days."

Sabrina jumped in immediately with "I don't think so, Nicholas. He made a couple of interesting points there. I always trust an expert who speaks 'from the gut'. The fact that Marco says these guys 'don't look like hunters' makes me suspicious myself. Who are they? What are they doing here? I'm sorry, I have to agree with Marco . . . something isn't right . . . and the way things are now . . . I doubly agree with him!"

Jake and Matt added their agreement to the argument. Both men knew what and who they were dealing with, and knew they had to acknowledge their suspicions based on their new-found information.

"Matt, who the hell could this be. Is somebody coming out here to do us harm. Would she go that far?" Jake asked.

"Yes, she would!" Sabrina jumped in. "How many times do you guys have to be told . . . nothing is beyond her reach!"

Elena moved a little closer to Matt. "Darling . . . I think you'd better listen to Jacques Manet's *'femme fatale'*. She might have a point there . . . I'm so glad she's on our side.*"*

Matt agreed, "Yes, my love." Turning to Jake he added "Jake, I think we'll call in a little extra security here. I'll have our guys from headquarters do a few patrols around the ranch on horseback. If they come across anyone, they can identify them and clear this up."

Jake looked across to Sabrina who was just sitting there, shaking her head.

§

By mid afternoon of the next day, there were two PFA officers riding around the ranch, enjoying what they thought was going to be a bit of a holiday. Nothing was heard from them for a couple of days, and Matt sent some others to check. They discovered sadly, that they hadn't survived the first day . . . their bodies were not discovered until two days later.

Matt called in all of the residents and the forensic crew from Buenos Aires for another summit meeting at the estancia. Some of the first clues learned were disturbing. Both men had died from a 9mm slug at close range through the head. Mateo and Jacques agreed this method resembled gangland style executions, very clean and final. They definitely were not 'hunting accidents. Nicholas and Paula were horrified, and so saddened by the deaths of the two young officers. They were too close in age to Mateo. The two parents realized just how dangerous their son's career could be.

Sabrina was diplomatic enough not to scream out 'I told you so!' to the rest of the gang, but knew within herself that this was just the beginning. At every opportunity, she tried to convince Jake just how serious the situation was, and remembering their common background and experience, Jake knew she was correct.

The ranch was put on alert, with strict orders for nobody to ride out alone, and if any strangers were encountered, caution should be strictly observed, and details relayed to the main house, where the PFA had set up a communications centre. Matt talked at lengths to his boss in Lyon, giving Jacques as much information as possible, as they tried vainly to tie this back to the 'Serbian Bitch'. Their only outstanding clue was a lengthy phone call from Dejana Babić to someone in Buenos Aires two days before. Jacques Manet was tracking everything he could, tracing the location of every Serbian gang member he knew of, and especially every Serbian in Buenos Aires

The entire atmosphere of their vacation at the estancia changed. The idyllic experience that Jake and Sabrina had enjoyed before had changed to a nightmare of suspicions, stress and fear for their life. Sabrina made sure her little Beretta Pico was always with her, and Jake had borrowed a 9mm Glock to carry as well. Matt of course, was never without his Bersa Thunder 9. Nobody was taking any chances of being surprised, and according to Sabrina's warnings and direction, they all became prepared and ready for a full out attack. She was much happier when the men allowed her to run a few 'defence courses' with everyone at the estancia.

At first, Matt was a little uncomfortable with a woman, Jake's girlfriend, taking charge of their defences and instructions. Elena soon convinced him that Sabrina was an experienced and highly skilled Swiss agent, with considerable training and talents of her own. "Just ask your boss, Jacques Manet", she told him. He finally relented and let Sabrina take over. As a back-up, he alerted his own office to have a special crew ready to be dispatched from either the main office or one of the provincial stations nearby. Jake and Sabrina knew they were asking for trouble and putting themselves at risk, but they agreed to remain enjoying their time on the patio. Even though they were exposed to more danger, they might draw out their opponent quicker by providing an easier target.

They didn't have to wait long. One evening directly after dinner, as they sat outside enjoying the cool air, Jake almost became the first casualty of their boldness. As he bent over to pick up his wine glass, he barely felt the wind of a high speed bullet as it passed within inches of his head. When the bullet hit the wine decanter on the shelf above him, glass and wine exploded around him.

"Everyone down!" he shouted, "This is it!" The entire gang went into their planned survival mode with a mad scramble for shelter. Then silence. Everyone froze, trying desperately not to make any noise as they listened for further attacks. Whoever had taken that shot, seemed to be farther away, as nothing happened for a short time. Seemed like forever to those hiding. Suddenly, all Hell broke loose and more bullets sprayed across the patio, missing the few still crouching flat on the ground. Everyone had an escape plan, and as the assailants closed in, Jake and the rest of them moved around behind trees and other protection, taking aim with whatever weapons they had. There were three men, all acting very confident as they approached the patio . . . one with a rifle, and the other two with automatic pistols, intent on eliminating them all.

Mateo jumped up and tried to slow down one of the assailants who was aiming his weapon towards Elena. The man turned and shot one burst, hitting Mateo in the shoulder, knocking him clear.

Sabrina jumped up and yelled "Hey! You big son-of-a-bitch!" The man turned and Sabrina's little Pico plugged a 38 calibre slug right between his eyes.

When Nicholas saw the other man heading towards Paula, he stepped right in his way and before the man had a chance to do anything, Nicholas' 12 gauge *escopeta* boomed, blowing a large hole in the man's chest.

The third man didn't have a chance. Before he could raise his weapon again, Marko and one of his men dragged him to the ground, beating him senseless. It was all over in minutes, and Mateo had the man in handcuffs and was on his phone as Elena treated his wounds.

Jake looked over the scene, amazed by what he just witnessed. He never got one shot away, it all happened so fast. He watched Sabrina, realizing it was the first time he had seen her in action. In addition to his deep love for this woman, he had an incredible sense of awe and pride for her.

He saw Paula hugging Nicholas, scolding him for being such a hero, yet thanking him for possibly saving her life. As Jake watched them, he had a feeling they had been through scenes like this before.

# Vengeance - Chapter - 30

It seemed like only minutes before the estancia driveway was plugged up with police cars, ambulances and emergency vehicles of all kinds. The paramedics looked over Mateo's wounds and wanted to take him to a hospital, but after much discussion and a heated argument, they decided he would survive with Elena's first aid. The two main casualties of the attackers did not fair as well. One had a small hole in his forehead, and the other had a large hole in his chest. The only one to survive was just regaining consciousness as the medics looked him over. Needless to say, he was a little surprised when he learned of their failed attempt to eliminate Jake and Matt. He then became agitated and appeared worried. Sabrina was watching and later told Jake and Matt that she had seen this before. With some gangs . . . failure to do your job was not acceptable and usually meant you were finished . . . one way or another. Sabrina also warned Matt to have his men keep a close watch on their prisoner, make sure he does not have access to anything to do himself in, otherwise they would never find out who hired him and his buddies.

Unfortunately, they ignored Sabrina's warning. When the police van carrying the man back to Buenos Aires arrived at the lockup, they found him lying in a pool of blood in the back of the van, with a very sharp pocket knife lying beside him and a severed femoral artery.

Needless to say, a few heads rolled and Mateo had a hard time explaining to Jacques Manet at Interpol how they managed to lose their first good chance to connect something to Beograd. Mateo was not only embarrassed, but very apologetic to Sabrina, who kindly enough, did not emphasize the 'I told you so' phrase. Elena was not as kind, giving Matt Hell every chance she got.

When the forensic team went over all of the victims, they discovered they all had Serbian passports, and had been in Argentina for several months. So they were not brought in just for this job, but most likely worked in the drug trade and this was just an extra which they thought would be easy money.

The next evening, they were once again gathered on the patio for dinner and drinks. Thankfully, all of the bodies had been removed and the blood and glass cleaned up. Sofia, the housekeeper appeared to take this in her stride, almost as if something like this happened every day. After a quiet dinner, Nicholas stood up, holding Paula's hand as they addressed the group. He was trying to appear serious and solemn, but a smile crossed his weathered face as he started "Well, *buena noches y bienvenidos,* good evening and welcome to you all . . . hopefully a much better evening than the last time we met here. We would like to assure our new guests, Sabrina and Jake, that this is not the way we normally run this estancia!"

This brought laughter all around. "But . . . I must add . . . it does show that any guests staying here are protected from any outside violence . . . even if they have to bring their own weapons!" looking directly at Sabrina. He started laughing and everyone joined him, Sabrina especially. "We, Paula and myself, would like to thank all of you for your help, with special thanks to Sabrina, our *'Mujer Maravilla'* or 'Wonder Woman' from Switzerland!"

Jake burst into applause, a feeling of pride and love exploding inside him as he watched Sabrina blush at all of the attention. Jake started to blush himself as he thought about how he was going to make love to this woman later that evening. He could hardly wait, and as he caught Sabrina's eye, she smiled back, knowing exactly what he was thinking.

§

The bottle of *Rakija* and some glasses exploded against the stone fireplace across the room when Dejana read her emails. She couldn't believe what she was seeing. The first item was a report on what had happened in Buenos Aires. How stupid could those guys be . . . attacking the group directly like they did? One of them had a rifle with a scope, he could've stayed back at a distance and picked them off one at a time. Even so, from what she learned, he missed his first shot which was supposed to finish Prescott. And then they stormed in, guns blazing, and ended up getting the same in return.

She talked a long time to her contact in Buenos Aires, Goran Ŝarić. She had known Goran for years, since he had managed to survived the narco mafia purge years before by Boris Tadić, who was Prime Minister at the time. Boris, and his Deputy Prime Minister, Ivica Daĉić mounted an all-out war on dozens of mafia operations, involving over a hundred arrests in Serbia, Croatia, Montenegro and throughout the Balkan states.

Dejana had chosen Goran as she thought he would be the perfect candidate to set up this hit on Prescott and his friends. Goran himself was equally pissed off at the results.

"I'm really disappointed in you, Goran" Dejana repeated, "I thought you, of all people, could handle a simple job like this."

"Hold it Janny," he started, using a pet name that Dejana was always a little touchy about. "I have in my hands a copy of the official police report covering that entire operation. We have a few discrepancies we need to deal with before you chew me out. First, you said they were just a scientist, a rancher and a local police officer. I wasn't too keen on the police officer thing, but you were paying the price, so I couldn't argue." He stopped, looking at the police report again, "But no, this so called scientist has a history with you, plus a lot of training in weapons and antiterrorism operations. He's not just your average science geek!" He continued to read "This police officer is actually head of his department at the PFA, and . . . and works for Interpol at their NCB in Buenos Aires."

Dejana cringed as she knew what was coming next.

"And . . . the simple girl friend . . . wow! . . . I'm surprised you didn't mention this one . . . she's a Swiss FIS agent, skilled as well in anti-terrorism, weapons trained . . . the whole thing!" He started to laugh over the phone. "We won't even start on those 'simple ranchers', they have been around the block, they are tough as nails, skilled and experienced at dealing with situations like this. It's no wonder they gave my men a run. I must say though, my guys were stupid to attack the way they did. That's the problem . . . too much muscle, not enough brains!"

Dejana was glad that he at least accepted some of the blame. "OK, so what do we do now? How am I going to get rid of this thorn in my side?"

"Let me think on it a while," Goran replied, "This is going to take more thought, planning, muscle and a lot more money!"

# Vengeance - Chapter - 31

Jake and Mateo took a long walk the next morning, not only to clear their heads, but to ensure their conversation was private. After they had walked for some time, Matt turned to Jake, who was hiking along with his cane, struggling to keep up. "So what's up Jake? You obviously wanted to get away from the house. What's on your mind?"

Jake paused, still wondering how he was going to bring up this subject. "Matt," he started "We've known each other for some time, even though we only recently reconnected."

"Oh, this sounds serious." Matt countered.

"Yeah, it is serious Matt, and I don't want it to get any more serious."

"What do you mean . . . more serious? A lively shoot-out on the patio is not serious enough?"

"No, no, that's not what I'm saying." He paused as he collected his thoughts. "Sabrina and I have had a wonderful time here, and appreciate you and Elena, and her parents inviting us to stay. It's been absolutely wonderful, more than we ever expected to enjoy on a vacation down here. But, I'm afraid we can't stay any longer. Sabrina and I have talked about this, and after that business the other evening, we realize we are putting all of you, the whole family at risk. These guys, under the direction of that woman in Serbia, are out to get us, myself in particular. I cannot in good conscience stay here and take the chance that they might attack again, with even deadlier force."

"Hold on right there!" Matt interrupted. "Before you get carried away with all these apologies and excuses, just think of this. I am a police officer of the Buenos Aires division of the Argentine Federal Police, as well as an Interpol agent in the Argentine NCB. In case you hadn't noticed, I am actively involved in this case, and have been even before you arrived." He held up his hand to stop Jake from interrupting. "So don't blame yourself or Sabrina for bringing this on. This is a police matter, and if you are involved in some way, 'suck it up'!"

Jake nodded in understanding. "O.K. Matt, but I just wanted to say this whole thing has changed a lot since we began with that environmental protest. The drug cartel involvement has increased and a completely different cast of 'bad guys' has entered the scene. This is not my area of expertise Matt . . . I'm an 'environmental' nerd!

"I realize that Jake, but we know that woman in Serbia is still behind a lot of this, and you do have some background with her, as well as a few debts to clear. So, I suggest we carry on. I still need your input and Sabrina's of course." Matt started laughing as Jake attempted to interrupt again. "No, seriously Jake, we'll work this out, and I'd appreciate your input and expertise and like I said . . . Sabrina's expertise." "So let's not hear any more about this, let's go back and have a beer and some lunch."

"That reminds me," Jake said, "Sabrina has some things she wanted to discuss with you and Nicholas."

§

Matt made sure both Nicholas and Sabrina joined them on their patio. The noon-day sun had warmed the area and large sun umbrellas were set up to provide some shade for the tables. Sofia had laid out a substantial buffet lunch on a side-board at the edge of the patio. Nicholas was showing off yet another of his new wines he had acquired during his recent trip to Mendoza. He went on at great lengths extolling the features of the wine, the bouquet, the palate, the lingering finish, mentioning the hints of this and that . . . traces of tastes most of his guests couldn't detect. His efforts were wasted on Matt and Jake as they each cracked open a cold beer.

Finally, when they were all seated with their food, Sabrina clinked her glass to get their attention. "Hi everyone. Jake and I were planning on telling you we were leaving. We didn't feel it was right, or safe for us to stay here attracting more attention and perhaps further attacks from undesirables."

She looked over to Jake and nodded. "But, fantastic hosts as they are, Elena, her parents and Matt have all convinced us to stay and fight it out . . . one way or another." She looked over to Nicholas and Paula, mouthing a 'thank you' to both of them.

"But," she continued, "I cannot stay without doing something further to protect all of us. I have given this a lot of thought, and as you know, I do have some experience with this type of criminal."

The small group hung on to her words, ready to take in whatever advice she was about to share. "First, Nicholas, I think this should be passed on to your foreman and any other lead hands you have on the ranch. And Sofia . . . please take a chair and listen. This involves your work as well."

Jake knew roughly what Sabrina was going to say, but he was also waiting to hear her 'words of wisdom'.

"First, the enemy we are dealing with is efficient, brutal, clever and uncaring about your laws or rules. They usually only have one goal in mind . . . to win! Most of them have experienced wars in their own country . . . wars of unspeakable cruelty and killing. In addition, they are most likely involved in the drug trade that involves so much money, profit, and high living, that some bending or breaking of the rules doesn't even slow them down." She paused, a look of genuine concern on her face. "As I was considering last night what to tell you, the most important detail I recalled was that these guys now have an extremely clever scientist behind them, a dedicated psychopath who is capable of devising poisons that are as sneaky as they are deadly. For that reason, you should not expect a direct frontal attack like the last one. I feel she is going to back off on the 'muscle' approach and use her other skills. Oddly enough, this kind of attack is more difficult to detect and defend." Sabrina paused, looking directly at Nicholas. "I don't know what may come next, but an attempt to poison everyone is not impossible. Nicholas, what is your water supply? Is it safe, secure from contamination, can it be accessed by outsiders? Maybe some guards should be posted at or near the well or water tower. These are the type of questions you must ask yourself. Also, food . . . this is a little more difficult to deal with for a mass poisoning. Air . . . we've already had the attempt with CO contamination, but don't be too complacent. They might think of another way to get at us." She stopped again, obviously disturbed by her own words. "And . . . worse case . . . if they get to us . . . what detection identification techniques do we have? Jake . . . do your lab guys in Vancouver have any detection methods or even antidotes for these poisons? We have to ask Alan Cook what he knows and what we should know about ricin, digitalis, abrin, tincture of oleander and others. I'm sure our gal in Serbia has tinkered with all of these. Alan has done some work on Tetrodotoxin and Batrachotoxin, but we need something that might be good for others. Even anthrax is a possibility." Every person listening looked at each other, shaking their heads as they contemplated what Sabrina was suggesting to them.

# Vengeance - Chapter - 32

Jake received a phone call from his Vancouver office during breakfast the next day. Alan Cook's British accent identified him before he had finished his first sentence. "I got your email last night Jake, along with your 'shopping list'. I'm afraid I don't have much help to offer you as far as your list of poisons."

"Surely Alan, there must be some identifying features of these poisons, and antidotes?"

"Maybe your Serbian problem has more on that, especially if she has been working with them for a long time and developing 'new and improved' versions." He stopped, hesitating to admit his own defeat. "We are just not equipped for this Jake. She is a highly trained organic chemist, also with long term experience and skills in botany. We can figure out some of it, which we did with the Batrachotoxin, but only with the help of our trusty GC Mass-Spec. And if we have an idea what to look, we can analyze certain samples, detect minute amounts, etc.. We don't have an easy detection method, especially for all these other things like abrin, ricin, maitotoxin and especially VX. For some, there is no antidote. Once it is in your system and symptoms start to appear . . . you're bloody well 'toast'! Some of them, like VX for instance, work on the nervous system, basically shutting things down. Others screw up your digestive system or your kidney function, with the same final result . . . note . . . emphasis on

*Final!* Jake, there are too many variations for us to mount any defence against. I haven't even mentioned Furocoumarins, the Cyanogenic glycosides, the Lectins and the Mycotoxins . . . some of these substances are around us every day, in things we see, use and eat, but all it takes is a slight variation in the genetic or chemical make-up, and *Voila*! . . . you have a deadly poison!" Alan paused, them said "Sorry chaps, but I'm afraid that awareness of your surroundings is going to be your best defence."

As Jake disconnected the call, he turned to the others around the breakfast table. "Well folks, you heard the man. I was afraid that's what he would tell us . . . we're on our own . . . no 'magic pill'.

§

Bert Jackson opened the file his secretary had dropped on his desk. He saw immediately it was from Jacques Manet in Interpol. Bert was a tall, African-American FBI Special Agent with an impressive record. He had worked briefly the previous two years, with Jacques Manet on cases involving an organization based in Europe who basically ran a 'murder for hire' business. They specialized in eliminating any scientist who preached the gospel about Global Warming. Too many large international firms were losing large amounts of money when people got too excited about the problems related to Climate change. Bert had been helping with whatever support the Bureau could offer to track down individuals or dig out details of their past and present activities. A lot of their work culminated with a major shootout in Bavaria two years ago and another serious confrontation last year in Bregenz, Austria. Bert had also helped Interpol track an individual with U.S. connections who was involved with a firm in Serbia run by a serious 'mad scientist' lady who was extremely skilled at poisoning people. Bert always called this woman the 'mad scientist' lady, but he knew others referred to her as the 'Serbian Bitch'.

Bert picked up the file and began to read the pertinent details. Although they had never been able to actually pin something on that woman legally, they all felt she was behind a lot of 'mysterious deaths' of important people, either scientists or politicians. Bert had that 'special feeling' he got whenever he felt he knew the answer to their problem. Jacques Manet was asking him for what ever information he could supply on Radomir Marković. Marković, aka Ray Marko, was a Serbian who had been living in California for a few years, since escaping from a questionable past involving the Serbian drug scene. Again, nothing specific that the FBI or immigration department could pin on him, but he had lived a clean life as a salesman and business manager since arriving in the USA. Bert had considerable experience with this kind of character, as well as these kinds of organizations.

He pushed his intercom button "Gladys... could you please bring me the latest INTERPOL – RHIPTO reports? Bert's work involved cooperation with Interpol and other organizations to track illicit money not only involving U.S Companies, but global organized crime. The World Atlas of Illicit Flows, compiled by INTERPOL – RHIPTO, a UN-collaborating centre, and the Global Initiative Against Transnational Organized Crime, provided him with the first consolidated global overview regarding conflicts worldwide. Of the USD 31.5 Billion in illicit flows generated in conflict areas, ninety-six percent goes to organized crime groups, to help fuel the conflicts!

"Here you are, Bert", Gladys said as she interrupted his reading, dropping another file on his desk. "It sounds like Jacques is getting a little concerned with this woman in Beograd. Apparently she's starting to get involved with that group down in Buenos Aires."

"Yes, Gladys. That concerns me. I don't want another so-called innocent US citizen using US laws to work around illicit dealings."

"That's something I don't understand, Bert," she answered, "I see this all the time on TV . . . the bad guys using 'shell companies' and other tax dodging schemes to disguise their activities and hide their money. Do you know how that works here in the United States?"

"Well Gladys . . ." Bert started, "It is all legal and above board . . . at least on the books. The 'bad guys', as you call them, can set up fake businesses to mask the true nature of their activities, and can also transfer money around the world. These fake businesses are called 'shell companies', all perfectly legal, but actually do not have any real operations, don't manufacture anything and don't provide any service."

"But . . . " interrupted Gladys again, "Isn't this all done somewhere in a foreign or tax haven country?"

"Yes. Places like Panama and the Cayman Islands are famous for that, but we have a huge amount of it going on right here in the US. US laws allow a veil of secrecy to mask many of the activities of these corporations . . . most notoriously in Delaware, Wyoming and Nevada. In these states, taxes are low and very little information is required to form a business."

"Surely they can't flaunt the laws and do things that are illegal." Gladys started.

"That's the problem. It's all legal and very difficult to track and control. Some of these shell companies have masked the activities of a Russian arms dealer, known as the 'Merchant of Death', selling weapons to terrorists."

"Oh My God!"

"Yes . . . and a few years ago the DEA discovered the Sanchez Paredes family behind the Peruvian drug trafficking ring, allegedly used a complicated combination of shell companies and gold mines in Peru to disguise their cocaines proceeds for decades . . . decades, Gladys!"

"I had no idea . . . and you deal with this all the time! I've worked with you for six months, so I guess I'd better start learning about this stuff!"

"I don't always let you in on the scary side of our cases Gladys, but yes, you should be aware of what's going on here and around the world." Bert stopped, then picked up the file from Interpol Gladys had given him this morning.

"That's why I want to pay particular attention to anything involving the Serbs at this point. Some time back, another of your 'shell companies' financed a Serbian crime boss tied to the murder of the country's Prime Minister. I want to really watch this Marković guy closely, and make sure we know what he is up to. They already have met him in Buenos Aires . . . and that scares me!"

# Vengeance - Chapter - 33

Bert Jackson spent most of the day studying the latest reports from Interpol. The FBI worked closely with Interpol, especially in the area of tracking money flow throughout the world. As the old rule states, "follow the money", and Bert knew it was more true now than ever.

He remembered a couple of years ago when agents and officials from over a hundred countries met in Toledo, Spain to call for better prevention, investigation and tracking to disrupt and ultimately prosecute those responsible for drug trafficking. National Central Bureaus gathered at the first INTERPOL Global Conference on Illicit Drugs to more efficiently tackle the trafficking of drugs. Some of the ideas implemented resulted in a seizure by Spanish authorities of nearly nine tonnes of cocaine, the largest cache of drugs ever seized in a single container in Europe.

Bert continued to read, always fascinated and horrified by the magnitude of the numbers. Numbers like 250 million drug consumers worldwide, resulting in economic benefits of over USD 300 billion per year.

Shaking his head, he skipped over the following pages of statistics to look at what was happening in the US – Argentina areas. Bert had a huge amount of respect for the Argentine PFA in Buenos Aires. As the Argentine Interpol NCB (National

Central Bureau), the PFA had recently arrested Hell's Angels member Paul Eischeid, a fugitive from California, wanted in the US for multiple crimes.

Another successful investigation by the NCB's in Washington, Buenos Aires and Montevideo led to the arrest of Bruce Vito Venero, wanted for drug trafficking, money laundering and jumping bail ten years earlier. He was the subject of one of Interpol's 'Red Notices'.

Buenos Aires' facial recognition system at the airports had also been very successful. He flipped through the pages, hoping to find some good news.

Before he got much further, his intercom pinged. "Bert" announced Gladys, "Speak of the devil . . . Jacques Manet from Interpol is on line one."

"Thanks, Gladys," as he picked up the phone. "Jacques . . . Bonjour, ça va?" Bert answered, almost depleting his knowledge of French.

Jacques answered with a laugh and a very English accent. "Jolly Good Bert, but your attempts at international diplomacy are wasted on me. I'm having trouble keeping up with American English"

"Well, I'll try to keep it simple then Jacques. How can I help you today and how are things in Lyon?"

"I've been going over some of the reports from the PFA in Buenos Aires, and I don't like what I'm hearing. Do you have anything further from your chaps you can add?"

Bert gave it some thought, also disturbed by the information about Marković in Buenos Aires. "No, Jacques, nothing specific, but I'm sure if he makes any moves, Mateo Perez will be on top of it."

"Yes, I know he'll have his eyes on Marković, but who else is operating there that we don't know of?"

"You're right of course Jacques, but we really can't do much right now. You keep in touch with Mateo a lot, don't you . . . as well as Jake Prescott from Vancouver? I learned recently he was there with his girl friend on vacation." He paused and added "That Prescott guy . . . I sometimes wonder about him," he laughed, "He seems to know exactly where the trouble is going to happen, or he is causing it!"

Jacques responded laughing. "There have been many times I've thought about that myself."

"I thought Prescott was an environmental scientist. How come he's getting involved with Perez on these drug cases?"

"Actually, just by chance. That woman in Serbia was financing the protesters in the environmental thing, and we suspect she was the one that had the politician killed during one of their protest meetings with the ranchers. In a very short time, this thing has just morphed out of shape, from an environmental activist problem to a major drug cartel problem."

"So, what now? We just wait and see?"

"Bert, are you sure this is a secure line?"

"Of course Jacques, it's a private extension in an FBI facility. I demanded a secure link when I took over this job, and it's checked every few days by our security and IT people."

"Jolly Good! Then I have something we should discuss between you and me. We might have an undercover agent that we could send to Argentina. He's not really an Interpol man, but has worked undercover with the Serbian Police, and a member of the International Police Association. I met him a while back at one of those international drug conferences. I've checked and he's really good at undercover work. He's kept a very low profile, so he's not well recognized by any members of the drug business."

"So what are you suggesting Jacques? Would he be good for the Buenos Aires thing?"

"That's what I'm thinking. I'm not sure how at this time, but we'll work on it and see if we can use him."

"OK Jacques, anything to keep our eyes on things. I get worried when I know someone's in town and I have no idea what they are doing."

"I'll be talking to Jake and Mateo as well . . . bring them up to speed and swear them to secrecy."

"Good."

"Right, Bert, Cheerio!" Jacques replied, wondering to himself if he was doing the right thing.

§

Jake and Mateo received the idea when Jacques phoned later that day. Both thought it could work, but only if the guy was good. Undercover work with these guys is a very dangerous game. You definitely don't want to get caught by some Serbian drug gangs, prying into their business dealings.

"Well, " said Jake, "If he's done this before, he could really help. I know nobody else but another Serb could pull it off."

So they gave Jacques the go-ahead to set up an undercover operation . . . slowly, discreetly, and only if the opportunities present themselves.

§

Jake and Mateo talked later, concerned about the new ideas and plans that Interpol was putting into action. Jake looked over to Matt, he was sure something was bothering his friend.

"What's up Matt? You don't look very happy about this. Is something bothering you?"

"No, it's OK Jake, I'm just concerned . . . anything could go wrong."

"Yes, we knew that. I'm sure Jacques has considered all this. We shouldn't try to figure it out."

"Something else is bothering you. Come on Matt, what is it?"

"Jake, I'm sorry. I should have told you a long time ago. but the 'need to know' group had to be very limited."

"What are you talking about Matt. What's going on?"

"Well, you have to keep this under your hat . . . not even tell Sabrina." He thought a minute and added "OK, I know that's not going to happen . . . but definitely nobody else."

"What the hell are you talking about Matt? Tell me straight up!"

"That undercover guy is already here, has been for some time. I only learned a short time ago Jacques has been working on some drug gang links around here for a long time, you know, the Argentine, Uruguay, Europe drug trade, major trafficking routes supplying the European market. He only managed recently to get this Serbian guy into the mix. I have no idea how he keeps track of him or if he's actually learned anything from him."

"Oh my God!" Jake breathed. "This could change everything. Do we know if he's working with any of the other Serbs . . . specifically those working for Dejana Babić."

"I have no idea Jake. Like I said, I only learned about this recently. I don't know how they have this guy set up, where he is, how he fits into the Serbian scene around here, or what. I work for Interpol and Jacques only let me know after some of these other things started to happen. Jacques didn't want us to check into certain things too far, we might 'upset the applecart' so-to-speak. We don't want to break his cover or put any suspicion on him at all."

"So what . . . we just sit back and wait for something to develop?" asked Jake.

"That's all we can do Jake. Wait until we learn something, or Jacques gives us some direction."

"I'm not very good at waiting." Jake answered.

# Vengeance - Chapter - 34

They didn't have to wait very long. A few days later, Mateo received a call from his office. All vacations had been cancelled and Matt was to report to the office asap! They were all having breakfast when the call came in, and turned to Matt with an unanimous question . . . "what the hell is going on"?

Matt answered with "I don't know, but it must be pretty serious! I've never seen them do this before. Something big must have happened. I'll call you as soon as I find out." With that, he was out the door with no further explanation.

Jake and Sabrina turned to their hosts and asked "Nicolas . . . Paula . . . do you know what is going on? How come Mateo was recalled from his vacation? Does this happen very often?"

"No!" they both answered. "This is the first time I've seen him so upset and determined to get to his office. Something *muy grande,* very big, must be happening and we're worried. It is probably dangerous."

"I have to agree with you." said Jake. "Elena . . . did Matt say anything to you? Do you have any idea what's happening?"

Elena was shaking her head, obviously upset herself with the events of the morning. "No, he didn't say anything, the first I knew was that call he received this morning. Jake, Sabrina, what's happening? I don't have a good feeling about this. How can we find out?"

"We probably can't get any information from the Buenos Aires office, or even the NCB. What ever is bothering them right now . . . they won't want to talk to us."

"But I think I know somebody who does know what's going on." said Sabrina. She and Jake were thinking similar thoughts, but were both stumped as to what could precipitate such action to involve the entire police department. The first thing that Sabrina thought of was to call Jacques at Interpol and see what he knew. If he already had a man on site, he might know what the situation was. Jake agreed, Jacques was most likely the best source of information. As a Swiss FIS agent, Sabrina was in a better position to request the information than Jake, who was only a civilian, despite of all the experience he had with the law enforcement agencies in the past few years.

Within minutes, she had Jacques on the phone . . . almost as if he was waiting for her call. "Sabrina, my dear, how are you . . . are you enjoying your vacation in Argentina?"

"Oh Jacques, *mon amour* . . ." she answered in the same loving tone. Without pausing, she immediately switched to a more aggressive approach. "Cut out the bullshit Jacques! You know why I am calling. What the hell just happened in Buenos Aires? Why was Matt recalled from his leave? what's going on? Should we be worried?"

"Oh my, so many questions. I'll start with the last one. Yes, you should be worried . . . we are still assessing the threats to foreign tourists as several have been attacked in luxury areas of Buenos Aires, stealing things like cell phones and high-end watches and jewellery. They are still looking for the gang members who recently shot a British tourist. Mateo should be able to fill you in on that file." He paused, and Sabrina could hear papers being shuffled. "I also learned why all your friends at the B&B are heavily armed. A few years ago there was a major war going on in the Pampas . . . this was during a financial crisis and before the big shakeup in the police department.

Gangs were wandering the pampas, stealing grain, slaughtering cattle and taking only the prime cuts. A couple of farmers lost almost forty cows in two weeks. Most of this was up near Arrecifes, a sleepy little town about a hundred miles north of you. That's when they all started arming themselves, not only to stop the stealing, but to protect themselves. So . . . my friends. . . the Pampas is not the peaceful countryside you thought it was."

"I think we learned all that a couple of weeks ago with that shoot-out we had here." answered Jake. And I'm sure that Matt is up to date and well advised of all these petty theft problems you've mentioned." He paused, then continued "But that's ancient history. Jacques . . . what's going on now in Buenos Aires that we don't know about? How come Matt was recalled and we haven't heard from him since?"

"I wish I could tell you more guys" said Jacques, "but we really don't know much. For once, Interpol doesn't have the intelligence gathering capability we should have on the ground. I've asked Bert Jackson of the FBI to keep his eyes open for any interesting developments. In addition to that, a major gang war between drug lords has broken out, and even more serious . . . we have no idea who all the players are. I think you know about the undercover man we had there. He was one of the first casualties. I don't know how they found out, or even if they did, but he got caught in the crossfire and was killed in the first salvo. We're still trying to figure it all out . . . that's why Matt was recalled. We need every man on deck to figure out what and who is involved."

"My God! This could be bad . . . real bad." Sabrina said, her voice low and controlled." Jake watched her, still spellbound by this beautiful creature who was so knowledgable in the ways of criminals, yet so loving and kind to him. Once again, he was glad he was on her side of the law.

Jacques continued slowly. "Sabrina, my dear . . . I'm not sure if I should even bring up the next subject, but, in your faraway fortress in Switzerland, have you ever heard of MS13?"

Jake could see Sabrina almost jump when she heard those words. He heard her small gasp of air as she started to answer Jacques. Slowly, she answered "Yes . . . Jacques . . . I have . . . " She glanced over to Jake, a worried look on her face. "What are you saying Jacques . . . are you saying they are involved somehow here?"

"That's the problem. We just don't know. They mainly operate out of El Salvador and the United States, and have recently expanded into Guatemala and Honduras. We know they have some activity in Italy and Spain . . . that's where we are getting some information that they might be moving into South America . . . Brazil, Uruguay and Argentina. We don't know any details other than that."

Sabrina turned to Jake again. "Jake, I think we should go home!" as she buried her head in her hands.

"Sabrina! What the hell! Who or what is MS13?"

"Jake . . . I hope you don't have to learn about them the hard way. The MS13 stands for *Mara Salvatrucha,* and they are one of the world's largest and most violent street gang cartels."

"How come I've never even heard of them before?"

"Oh Jake . . . you are so innocent some times . . . you and your environmental crusade. You probably wouldn't learn about this group unless you were in the law enforcement business or one of their victims."

"Now you're making me feel bad. Just who and how big is this gang?"

"They started back in the 1980's in Los Angeles, and have spread to more than a half-dozen countries. They've become a central focus of law enforcement world-wide. Some organizations, like Interpol and FBI, figure MS13 has between 50,000 and 70,000 members."

"Holeee Sh . . ."

"Yes, my sentiments exactly!" Sabrina responded. "Not only that, they have a completely different type of organization . . . a loose collection of *clics,* or cliques, a community of people working loosely towards the same goal, with no appointed leader or even specific rules to follow. They run their organization under various 'guidelines', often with direction from jailed members based in whatever country they are operating in. They and their operations are a lawmaker's nightmare!"

"I had no idea!" Jake added. "Now I understand why you reacted to Jacques' words the way you did . . . but you didn't really mean we should go home, did you?"

"No Jake. It was just a normal reaction to Jacques' question. I don't think we should leave until we find out more from Matt. I feel we're obliged to stay and help, at least I am, being a law enforcement officer. We really shouldn't leave him now, even if we aren't part of his force."

Jake agreed, "No, of course we can't just drop everything and leave. But I feel that I am becoming more useless by the day. You and Matt are so familiar with this drug scene and street gangs, an area I know nothing about. All my environmental expertise is basically useless here.

# Vengeance - Chapter - 35

Mateo cursed again. He poured another cup of coffee, then changed his mind. He dumped it into the sink and brewed a *Mate* instead. The news of the undercover Interpol agent's death had dealt a crippling blow to their plans to infiltrate some of the drug organizations in the country. He had begun to feel they might make some progress in controlling the drug trade, but once again, the drug cartel's size, complexity and ruthlessness overcame the police's slow, measured approach to crime fighting. He could feel his anger rising, as well as his frustration at not being able to take action, action like moving in and wiping them all out in a massive shoot-out! As much as he'd like to do that, it was just a Hollywood pipe-dream, something that never really takes place, but is therapeutic to dream of it.

Back to the paperwork on his desk, he shuffled through various notices from Interpol and the FBI. Most of them said the same thing, nothing specific to report, but all containing a general overall feeling that something was going on, something big!

"*¡Mierda!* Bull Shit!" he screamed as he threw the reports across the room. Alarmed, his secretary came to the door. "Matt, are you alright? What's the problem?"

"I'm sorry Martina, but these reports tell us nothing! What the hell is wrong with everybody? Doesn't anyone know what the hell is going on?"

"I'm sorry sir, I just give you what comes in . . . from the usual sources."

"I know, Martina, I'm sorry, it's just that this whole thing is getting to me and I don't have any answers, and these reports are not giving me anything to go on!"

Martina was a very clever secretary, one who had been working in the business for quite a few years, and was not afraid to speak up. "Well, Señor Perez . . ." she always used 'Señor Perez' when she wanted Matt to listen closely. "First, I think you are spreading yourself too thin."

"What do you mean by that?" Matt asked.

"Well first, you're working on at least two major problems. The first is this big drug cartel thing, and the second, you're still working on this Serbian woman problem with Jake Prescott. I'm not surprised you're getting frustrated. As far as the first thing is concerned, the drug cartels, I think all these reports are from big organizations who haven't a clue about what is really going on. What you need is someone on the street, someone in the business who has 'his ear to the ground'! You know that's the only way you are going to get real, actionable intelligence. Who knows? You might find out information about both projects." She then added "You know people like that don't you?"

As soon as Martina said those words, Matt realized what he must do. "Of course I do Martina . . . thanks for jogging my memory . . . I know just the guy who might be able to fill in some blanks!" He looked again at Martina. "You said two things, what are your recommendations about the second?"

"Well, to me, it appears that your lady in Beograd is pulling the strings on these Serbian puppets here. They are mainly into the drug business, but they are taking orders from her. Most likely just doing other 'chores' for her to make a little extra money. Your friend Jake is an environmental expert, but these guys are not. They are just using brute force to get the job done. I think that's why things don't always seem to be logical . . . they are not . . . they are just impulse moves. You and Jake work with logic, so the whole thing confuses you!"

§

It was almost noon the following day before Matt managed to find his man and arrange a meeting. Joaquin Garcia was a small time burglar and street thug that associated with the one that Matt had arrested after his amateurish attempt to scare Sabrina and Jake out of town by breaking into their hotel room. Matt had had some dealing with this man before, and knew he was 'up' on all of the happenings at street level throughout Buenos Aires. After he had arrested his buddy Pedro, Matt put pressure on Joaquin and made a deal with him to supply information whenever Matt wanted it . . . information about things happening on the street.

Joaquin was very uncomfortable meeting directly with Matt in public. From experience, he knew that any dealings directly with the police usually ended poorly. His shallow breaths, sweaty palms and shaky voice told Matt that the entire operation could be in jeopardy if Joaquin could not control his emotions. Matt was dressed very casual, and he had chosen a bar far away from Joaquin's normal haunts. Even so, the flicker of his eyes and constant glances over his shoulder indicated Joaquin's concern.

"Jeez, Perez, this is crazy, meeting with you! If anyone sees us, I'm finished on the streets!

"Relax Joaquin, we've taken enough precautions, and I think we'll figure out a better system for you to get me information."

"And for you to pay me." Joaquin added.

"Of course," Matt agreed. "Now . . . here's what I am looking for." Matt continued, listing some of his concerns and information he was hoping to learn. Joaquin listened, thinking only about how much money he could make off this deal. Until Matt mentioned the name MS13.

"*¡Mierda!* Shit! Forget it!" Joaquin screamed as he jumped up from the table and turned towards the door.

Matt grabbed his jacket and pulled him back, forcing him to sit down in front of him. "*¡Cállate!* Shut up! Keep your voice down, idiot!" Matt hissed. "Do you want everyone here to notice, to pass on what they saw and heard? Now sit down and pull yourself together. You obviously have heard about these guys. What have you heard? That's all I want to know."

Joaquin was sweating even more now. He was visibly shaking, his head twisting back and forth to check every corner of the bar.

"Relax," Matt tried to calm him. "There's nobody here, the bar's almost empty, you haven't said anything that is going to get you into trouble! Pull yourself together for Christ sake!"

Joaquin slowly calmed down, realizing he was safe, but still very hesitant to talk to Matt. Matt continued "All I want to know is what have you heard about this organization. Are they operating here in Buenos Aires? Who is? How many? You know, things like that. I'm not asking for any trade secrets for Christ sake!"

"But . . . but . . . actually . . . I know nothing!"

"You know nothing, or you don't want to tell me anything. Which is it?"

"Both! All I have heard is stories about them . . . their reputation, how big their network is, how they treat people who work against them or double-cross them."

"Yeah, I've heard a lot of stories like that too." said Matt, but I think most of those stories are bullshit! Just stuff to scare guys like you."

"I don't know Perez, I heard it from a few good sources . . . it's real!"

"Good! I'm glad you have some 'good sources'. So tell me, what's going on? Is this outfit operating here? What are they up to?"

"I don't know for sure. All I've heard is they are thinking about it. You know, starting to gather their troops." He glanced around again, just to make sure they were alone. "That's all I know man . . . but I do know the other gangs are worried. There could be a lot of trouble, especially if the Serbs get pissed off."

"Thanks Joaquin. That's all I wanted to know, for now. Just keep your ear to the ground, let me know if anything changes. Now . . . let's figure out a system where we can communicate and where we can meet next time."

# Vengeance - Chapter - 36

Jake and Sabrina were going crazy back at the *estancia*. They hadn't heard anything from Mateo all day, and any calls to his voicemail were ignored. Nobody in his office was letting out any news, even when Elena called. As far as everyone was concerned, he didn't exist!

Matt had sworn everyone in his office to secrecy, told them not to give out any information . . . to anyone! Just plead ignorance and say he is out of the office and is not available, and he was not answering his cell phone. He did not want any leaks, no matter how small, nothing to leak out that might jeopardize what he was trying to do. They had already lost one undercover person before he even got started! He didn't want to lose another one.

He thought about his meeting with Joaquin Garcia, and felt it could work . . . Joaquin was greedy enough to overcome his basic fears of retribution and supply Matt with the information he needed. Besides, it was all low, street level information he wanted, not necessarily high end stuff from the cartels.

§

Joaquin Garcia had finally regained control of himself. After he had left Perez and walked a devious route to make sure he wasn't being followed, he finally arrived at his favourite bar near Plaza Dorrego in the San Telmo district. A quick double brandy, then he settled in a corner table with his favourite Fernet and cola. Slowly, as the alcohol did its job, he came back down from his heightened state of alert, almost panic. As he reviewed his meeting with Perez in his mind, he slowly realized he could have a good thing going here. He really didn't have to put himself at risk at all . . . just keep his eyes open and his ear to the ground, and report anything unusual. And the extra money, he could almost feel the bills in his hands, and the goodies it could buy. With a smile on his face, he ordered another drink.

§

It was late that day when Matt finally returned home to the *estancia*. He was almost trampled with enthusiastic greetings and a barrage of questions.

"Jeez Matt, you've be AWOL for almost two days! What the hell is going on?"

"Hold on . . . please let me get in and sit down! Elena, would you please pour me a drink? A good stiff one, if you don't mind."

"I'll get you one."Jake quickly offered. "And I'll join you." Soon, the four of them were sitting around comfortably in the great room, all staring at Matt, waiting for the big disclosure or explanation of his mysterious absence for more than a day.

"Well, I'm sorry folks, but I was not going to take any chances on someone overhearing my plans. I didn't want to put any of you at risk. So rather than take the time to explain it to you, I thought it would be better just to go ahead and explain later."

"Explain what?" they all chimed.

"OK, here it is." Matt looked around, glancing around, checking to see if they were alone and nobody else was close enough to hear what he had to say. He continued with an account of his actions and plans for using this Garcia character as an 'on the street' lookout, someone who could just keep them informed about any changes going on at street level.

"But I thought that was what Jacques was doing through Interpol." asked Jake.

"Yes, that was the plan. You saw how that turned out. I'm not going to infiltrate any gangs, nothing so covert or dangerous. Just another street level observer that can keep us informed of any changes that happen. We really need some kind of down-to-earth intelligence, and this is the only way I can convince someone to work with us . . . with little or no risk to him."

"Well, I suppose under the circumstances, that's the best we can hope for."

"Well, yes. Already Joaquin has indicated that there are some worries amongst the gangs about this big organization setting up here. They are all hoping they don't clash with the Serbian guys . . . we could have a bloodbath on our hands."

"Matt" started Jake "I've been sitting here cooling my heels most of the day, but I've been trying to catch up on the news, both online and with an English language newspaper that Elena got for us. I've been reading about all the troubles up in Rosario. That's not far away, is it, just up the road a few miles?"

"Yes Jake, not too far away, but a world away as far as what you are used to. Rosario is almost the hub of crime . . . the centre of the drug gangs and activity."

"I was reading about the GNA, the *Argentine National Gendarmerie*. Who the hell are they? How many police organizations do you have down here anyway?"

Matt laughed. He understood what Jake was asking. "Oh Jake, I realize that's what it sounds like, but believe me, each of these branches of our law enforcement has their own goals and responsibilities." He paused, taking another sip from his drink. "God, I needed that!" he mumbled.

"Starting with Interpol, you know them. They are our international link to other law enforcement organizations around the world. It's how we keep track of the 'bad guys', who's doing what, where they are, and who's wanted the most."

Jake nodded, very familiar with the operation of Interpol.

"Our own police force, the one I work for mainly is the Argentine Federal Police, the PFA, *Policía Federal Argentina*. We are the national civil police force of the Argentine Federal Government. We have operations throughout the country, and until just a few years ago, we were the local law enforcement of Buenos Aires."

"O.K., I understand that," said Jake, "But what is this other one, The *'Argentine National Gendarmerie'*, I've been reading about in this newspaper, this one over in Rosario? Sounds like the French 'Gendarmes'."

Matt laughed, realizing how confusing the whole thing could be to someone unfamiliar with the organization. "Well Jake, that's a horse of a different colour, I think you guys might say. First, regarding the 'Gendarmes', you have to remember that French and Spanish are both Romance languages, their roots in Latin, so you'll always see similarities. Just ask Sabrina. They have to deal with about four languages in Switzerland, but both French and Italian come from the same roots, as does English. German is another matter, which I'm sure Sabrina can explain better than I. These guys are our border police, to put it simply. The *Gendarmeria Nacional Argentina,* or GNA. It's a fairly big organization, more than 70,000 members, and operate as our frontier guards. They cover our borders with Brazil, Paraguay, Chile and Uruguay. They have five regional headquarters spread around the country, one of which for Santa Fe Province, is in Rosario. That's probably why you were reading about them with the news from Rosario. They are heavily involved in preventing smuggling, drug trafficking, terrorism, and crimes against the population like trade in humans, organs, slaves, and children. They also are deployed for military operations like the Falklands war, UN peacekeeping, etc."

"Well, O.K., I understand now why they could be so busy, especially if this Rosario is as notorious as you say."

"Even more so!" agreed Matt. "For instance, the homicide rate in Rosario was about three times the national average. This is mainly due to the drug trade, not only in Rosario, but in the entire province of Santa Fe, which had over thirty-two ports through which the drug traffic moves. To make things worse, each time the government or law enforcement cracks down on the trade, in only serves to fill or overload the prisons . . . prisons that were already filled with gang members and others running their organizations from the safety of their cells. In Rosario, more than twenty percent of the province's five thousand prisoners are held in police stations. Here in Buenos Aires, more than thirty-thousand prisoners are held in a space designed for twenty-six thousand."

"Why were you watching him for that long?" asked Jake, not familiar with a lot of police techniques and long term surveillance.

"Several years ago, Goran Ŝarić managed to avoid capture during a narco mafia purge by the Prime Minister Boris Tadić and his Deputy Ivica Daĉić. That purge rounded up hundreds of fairly high level narco mafia types throughout the Balkans. We never really had anything on Ŝarić, but we were pissed that he 'got away'.

"And, interrupted Matt, "We been looking for him ever since we first knew he was here. I guess that's another reason I'm a little worried. When someone disappears shortly after arriving, and we can't find him. I can't be sure he's not up to something."

"Right-O!" echoed Jacques. "The last known contact we had here was in Beograd, just before he arrived in Buenos Aires. Does that sound suspicious or what?"

Jake and Sabrina both nodded and agreed. "We think he just got his orders from the boss and has come here to do nasty things. Most likely to us, or Jake in particular."

"I think that's a good guess" agreed Matt, "at least it's a safe way to think for now. This means we have to find him, or at least be prepared for some action from him in the meantime. Santiago, my right hand man in the office, is tracking down some leads. He thinks he might know where Goran is and maybe even what he's up to!"

"Great! We can use all the help we can get." said Jacques. "And I think you guys are in a better position than me to find out where he is. That's your territory.

§

Jacques hung up the phone and decided to head home. It had been a long and tiring day, too many international puzzles bouncing around in his head with very few solutions to solve them. He almost reached his car in the parking area, when Malina Aleksov, his Serbian translator, exited from the shadows and approached him.

Surprised, he exclaimed "Malina! What? Why are you here, what's going on?"

"Please Jacques . . . can we get into your car?"

"Of course," he agreed, unlocking his car so they could both get in.

"I was hoping you would not work late tonight," she said as she entered the car. "I had to talk to you, and I couldn't trust doing it in the office."

"What, why?" asked Jacques. "My office is perfectly safe."

"Maybe" Malina said, "But I couldn't take a chance. I wanted to talk to you in private . . . real private! Please drive." she said, glancing around nervously. Jacques could see she was desperate, obviously worried that somebody would learn of their meeting. He pulled out of his parking lot and headed along *Quai Charles de Gaulle*. The traffic had not yet reached the

# Vengeance - Chapter - 37

Sabrina had been listening to all of this from Matt, much of which she was already familiar with. Her time and training with the Swiss Police had given her a good background about what Matt had just told them. Although these details were specific to Argentina, Sabrina knew how to apply her knowledge to other jurisdictions, so she immediately understood the overall drug route/gang problems they were experiencing and crime in this relatively small city of Rosario.

To expand on what Matt had told them, Sabrina also had some additional emails from Jacques, giving her some extra background on the problem. Sabrina shook her head, putting down the latest email from Interpol, an email that had just confirmed most of the information Matt had explained to them earlier.

The last email caught her eye. It was a copy of a quick note to Matt to stand by for a conference call regarding our 'current problem'.

§

Sabrina quickly checked with Jake and Matt to see if they knew what time Jacques was calling to discuss their 'current problem'. From what she could determine, Matt already knew what was happening, something he and Jacques had already discussed and were both working on.

"Soooo?" cried Sabrina. "Is anyone going to tell me what is happening?" She looked over to Jake, who didn't seem to know what was happening either.

"Relax Sabrina, Jacques is calling in just a few minutes. It's about someone we picked up on our airport facial detection system a couple of weeks ago." He made a face "as they say, he was a 'person of interest'."

"So, what's new? Where is he? Why are you interested in him now?"

"That's the problem. We don't know where he is, or what he's up to! That's why Jacques is calling . . . maybe he's got something."

"So who is this guy? Why are you interested in him?" asked Sabrina.

"I was hoping Jacques would have called by now, he could tell you." Matt started. "His name is Goran Ŝarić."

"The name sounds familiar," started Sabrina, "but all those Serb names sound alike after awhile."

"Well, my dear, this one has not only been involved in the drug trade, but is very close to our gal in Beograd . . . Dejana Babić.!"

Sabrina suddenly realized the importance of finding this guy. Characters like him should not be wandering around 'unescorted'.

Within minutes, Jacques Manet called. Matt set up the phone so they could all participate in the conversation. "*Buenos Tardes* to all of you in Argentina. How are things down there?"

"Fine Jacques, we've been waiting for your call. I hope you have some information for us."

"Not really, Matt. We had been watching Ŝarić for some time. Actually for a few years. So we were a little surprised when you guys picked him out with your facial recognition system when he arrived in Buenos Aires."

rush hour volume, so he kept glancing at Malina as he drove. Shortly along the *Quai,* he pulled over into the Tour bus parking area in front of the *Musée d'Art Contemporain.*

"O.K. Malina, let's have it! What's on your mind . . and why the 'cloak and dagger' routine?"

"Oh, Jacques, I'm so worried . . . you know who . . . she's given me an ultimatum."

"What do you mean, an ultimatum?"

Malina started crying, her composure broke down. Jacques watched as the poor girl was obviously terrified. He suddenly realized what a strain she had been under all this time, living her double life as an Interpol translator and informant, as well as under pressure to be an undercover Serbian assassin.

"Now, now . . . " he tried to comfort her, wishing his secretary, Annette was here. Annette was always good at calming the girl's worries and helping to overcome any concerns about her double life.

"No Jacques, you don't understand, I'm not concerned about myself. It's you, she wants to kill you! She wants me to kill you!"

Jacques wasn't surprised. This had happened before and he was expecting again. "Now, Malina, she wanted this before, we really shouldn't be surprised that she would ask again."

"No, you don't understand. This time she won't take no for an answer, no excuses. Otherwise . . ."

Jacques waited. "Otherwise? What Malina, otherwise what?"

"Otherwise she will kill either me or my aunt in Beograd!"

"Oh dear." mumbled Jacques, not sure how to handle this turn of events. He knew he had to have some support on this. "O.K., " he started "We'll talk about this in the office tomorrow . . . believe me, it is secure, nobody can spy on us. We'll ask Annette what she thinks, I'm sure she will have some ideas."

# Vengeance - Chapter - 38

They met the following morning at Interpol Headquarters, in a secretive and rather gloomy atmosphere in a small corner office, quite separated from where Jacques normally worked. Annette joined them, as well as another of Jacques' close associates, Pierre Dupuis. Pierre was a Cyber and communications expert, and had been used in the past to monitor Malina's communications with the Serbian Bitch.

Jacques started by greeting them all, with a special salutation to Malina. "Good morning Malina, I hope this location will satisfy your concerns about security. Hardly anyone uses this office and it is not associated with either of us in a work capacity." Turning to the others, he added "You already know Annette, my secretary. I think you also know Pierre Dupuis from communications, who I have asked to join us for reasons which will become apparent soon."

Malina looked around, studying each of the attendees at length. Jacques knew immediately something had happened since they had talked in the carpark the day before.

"Malina, what's the problem, dear? We talked about this yesterday. Has something else happened? Something we don't know about?"

"Oh Jacques, yes, she called me last night."

Pierre interrupted with "What? When? How come I was not aware of this? We've been monitoring your calls."

Malina responded. "My regular phone yes, but she gave me another phone . . . just for our private conversations . . . that's how she gave me the order to kill Jacques. She called me on it last night." She was obviously very disturbed, nervously shaking and close to tears. "Jacques . . . she asked me why I got into your car yesterday . . . where did we go?"

Jacques was shocked, realizing immediately what that meant. Someone within the organization was observing their actions and reporting back to that bitch! "O.K.," he started, "This puts a whole new face on our problem . . . we have a traitor . . . a mole in the organization." He looked around the table, only two other people, Malina and himself. He felt comfortable that the mole was not in this group. "So, Malina, what did you tell her?"

"I told her you just gave me a lift over to the Modern Art Museum, where you let me off. You were going in that direction anyway."

"Good! Let's hope she was satisfied with that." He turned to Pierre and added "Pierre, can you do your tech thing and cover Malina's extra phone as well, without anyone knowing it?"

"Yes, of course Jacques, I'll get on it right away. I didn't realize she had that one."

"Malina, you're going to have to tell us these things. If she gives you another phone, or some other way to communicate, we must stay on top of this.

Malina nodded, glad she had told them about the phone, and the spy in the organization. With that out of the way, she visibly started to relax. Jacques realized the girl must have been under considerable strain and stress from her dealings with the woman in Beograd. Annette could also see the difference in Malina's demeanour, and flicked a surreptitious glance over to Jacques.

"O.K.," started Jacques, "I think Malina, you should tell us as much as you can about what our lady in Beograd has asked of you."

Malina appeared cautious, glancing around at the others, even though she knew them all. Slowly, she looked at her hero, Jacques Manet, and started. "As you all know, we . . . myself, Jacques and this terrible woman in Serbia have been playing this dangerous game for the past year. We . . . I knew it was a tricky situation, but I felt I had it under control." Turning to Pierre she added "Pierre . . . you've been monitoring some of my communications, but not all. I still get emails, text messages and calls at home from her, mostly just family greetings, etc., supposedly from my aunt. They all come through on the phone she gave me, the one you said you can monitor now. We have sort of a code worked out . . . names for certain people . . . like you Jacques, that Jake Prescott in Buenos Aires. We even have a code for Buenos Aires, that's just BA." She smiled and added "I know, not very clever, but we sort of devised this on the go."

They all smiled and tried to encourage her to continue. "Recently, she has been getting very frustrated. First, she still hasn't been able to deal with Jake Prescott, her number one concern. Then Jacques, another thorn in her side. All of her plans have been spoiled, in may cases by amateurs, people who should be no problem for her, should not get in her way."

Jacques jumped in at this point with "Wait a minute, I take offence to that observation. I consider myself to be a consummate professional, not an amateur!"

They all laughed nervously, and turned back to Malina to hear what else she had. "She has recruited some pretty mean guys from the Serbian gangs and still has not made any headway."

"Yes Malina, we've been watching this unfold, especially down in Buenos Aires. So what now? She's decided to try something different?" asked Jacques.

Malina was almost in tears again. Annette went over and sat beside her, trying to provide a little comfort and support from an older woman. "Yes, it was just recently, maybe after another failure in Buenos Aires, she called me at home and asked if she could talk seriously. Of course I said yes, not realizing what she was going to ask. Basically, she wants to 'dispose of you' . . . her words, not mine, 'dispose of' Jacques Manet."

She looked over to Jacques, tears in her eyes. "Oh Jacques . . ."

Jacques jumped in immediately with "Malina! Don't be so upset girl. You haven't done anything wrong. There's nothing to be upset about. We'll work this out."

"But Jacques, she wants me to kill you, to poison you like those other poor people last year."

Annette tried to calm the girl, holding her hand tightly. "Now, Malina, stay calm. You're with friends here, you have the full support of Interpol behind you, Just think about that a moment."

"I have thought about it Annette, and I appreciate what you are saying, and the support you are all trying to give me." She sobbed again, and added "But she wants me to kill Jacques, who has helped me and been a good friend to me, even when I didn't deserve it!"

Jacques watched this play out, appreciating what his secretary was trying to do. He realized he had to try something different. "O.K., Jolly Good!" he began, "there you have it then . . . you'll just have to do what she has asked. You must kill me!"

They turned to him with mixed looks of confusion and surprise. Nothing was said for several seconds. Annette was the first to catch on, having worked with Jacques for many years, she knew how his mind could work, how devious this man could be. How else did he become the success at Interpol that he was?

"Yes, I agree" She smiled at Jacques. "Jacques Manet must die!"

At first, Malina looked horrified, then as another possibility sank into her mind, she smiled and looked at them all with a wrinkled brow and pouty lips. "Are you suggesting . . .?"

"Yes, Malina, we must figure out a way for me to die, or at least appear to die." He paused, and added "but it must be good . . . realistic . . . and very secretive. We can't have anyone thinking I am not dead, especially since she has someone watching us."

Annette turned to Pierre. "What do you think Pierre, you are the communications guy. Do you think we could pull off something like this?"

"Well, we'd have to have a few more people involved, but yes, I think we could pull off a very realistic murder of M. Jacques Manet. It might even work to our advantage . . . having a spy on board to report back to you-know-who!" Turning to Jacques he asked "Jacques . . . is there somewhere you can disappear to for a short vacation or something?"

"Yes," Jacques replied. "I think that can be arranged. As a matter of fact, I'm overdue for a vacation."

"It will have to be very secret, mind you, nobody must learn or even suspect you are still alive, especially if we have a resident spy on board!"

Jacques finally brought their meeting to and end with "O.K., there is a lot to think about and plans to be made. Let's all sit on this. I for one have a lot of work to do before 'I die'. Malina . . . you carry on as usual . . . don't worry about it, but if you talk with Dejana in the near future, just indicate you are are willing to comply.

# Vengeance - Chapter - 39

Jake was becoming more frustrated each day. He was not used to just sitting around, waiting, and he didn't even know what he was waiting for. He was a scientist, a chemist and a computer nerd. For years, almost all of his working life, he had used his intellect, his knowledge and especially his innate puzzle solving skills . . . to see patterns where others failed. None of these skills seemed to be useful in the present situation. He had always depended on his logic, but the pieces of this puzzle were so disjointed, so weird and unrelated, he was having trouble even keeping them all in his mind, let alone putting them together in an organized manner.

Sabrina looked at Jake, knowing he was getting stretched thin. "Jake," she asked "you can't figure out them all Darling, there are too many pieces to this puzzle, and there are too many different people, countries and motives driving them. You can't expect to solve it all, there is nothing to solve here, just a lot of bad people doing bad things to either make money, or just to survive."

"I know all that Sabrina, but we've got to make some sense out of it, try to figure out what the next moves are going to be."

"The next moves by whom?" Sabrina asked. "You see? That's the problem . . . you can't even determine who is going to make the next move."

"I can't just lie back and do nothing Sabrina. Matt's up to his ass with all this, and we're just complicating his life by just being here! We know Serbian drug gangs are moving in, as well as this other 'super' street gang operation, but we can't do much about that . . . that's Matt's and a P.F.A. problem." He stopped, hungrily staring at his beautiful Swiss powerhouse of a woman, wishing he was back in Vancouver with her, either hiking the North-shore mountains, or sailing the Salish Sea. Better still, making love to her in his apartment, something he planned to do as soon as they returned to Vancouver. He realized that was a dream. He couldn't leave all this to his friend Matt, seeing that he brought many of these problems with him, however innocently. He pulled himself together, looked again at Sabrina and announced "and as for that Serbian Bitch, I have to talk to Jacques again, and my people in Vancouver. We have to come up with something to protect us. Some kind of defence."

Sabrina nodded, knowing they had talked about this before and came up with nothing. This woman with her extensive repertoire of exotic poisons, made a realistic defence almost impossible.

§

A day later, all their worries and plans changed. Matt arrived home and as soon as he was in the door, he called them all together for the bad news. "I don't know how to tell you this guys . . . but our friend and colleague Jacques Manet is dead!

"What . . . how?" a collective gasp came from the group. Jake jumped up and almost yelled at Matt "No . . . what are you saying Matt . . .when did this happen . . . how?"

"It just happened, early this morning. Lyon is about four hours ahead of us, and it happened shortly after he came to work."

"How?"

"They think a heart attack. Jacques has been under a lot of stress lately." Matt shook his head. "God . . . I didn't think he would go this way, he was such a vibrant character!"

Sabrina glanced over to Jake, motioning him over closer to her. "Jake, are you thinking the same thing I am?" she whispered.

Jake looked at her and answered quietly "God, I'm pretty sure we're thinking along the same lines, my dear. I'm willing to bet this was not your ordinary heart attack. We have to find out, see the results of the autopsy . . . I'm sure there will be one."

After the initial shock of the announcement had worn off, Sabrina and Jake took Matt and Elena aside and shared their thoughts. "We think Madam Dejana had a hand in this." Jake said.

"I was wondering about that on the way home" Matt agreed. "You knew him personally better than I, but I always though he kept himself in pretty good shape."

"He did, he was fit as a fiddle, as they say at home! And although he took the job seriously, he never let it get to him." Jake added.

Matt then said "They are all pretty sad about it at work, at least those who had any dealings with him. This sophisticated 'English Bloke', with a very French name."

After a short pause, Jake announced "That's it then . . . I'm afraid Sabrina and I must say farewell and thank you and your parents for your hospitality, but we must leave. We will be going to his funeral, wherever it is, and I have to visit his family. We never knew much about his family . . . he was very private man, but we must pay our respects. I owe a lot to Jacques for what he has done for me in the past couple of years."

"But, you can't go." pleaded Elena.

"We must Elena . . . don't you see? If you have us . . . we will come back when things return to normal, whatever that is. I hope we'll be welcome then, and we promise not to bring the 'hounds of Hell' with us next time."

With some very short goodbyes to Elena and her parents with promises to return, Sabrina went directly to their room to pack while Jake got on the phone to call his office and make flight arrangements.

It was still morning in Vancouver when Jake called his office. Shannon had already heard the news from Interpol. "I'm so sorry Jake . . . I know how much he meant to you . . . especially after he tracked you down to that hospital in Germany after you were shot on that river barge."

"Yes, Shannon, just thinking about that brings tears to my eyes . . . he was a good man. Can I talk with Alan please?"

"Yes, he's right here."

"Jake, I'm so sorry about Jacques, but I want to talk to you about that."

"Are you thinking what I'm thinking Alan?"

"I think our Serbian bitch had a hand in this, Jake. I don't know how . . . but I'm willing to bet on it."

"My thoughts exactly Alan, maybe the autopsy will show something."

"If it's what I'm thinking, they will only detect it if they use some very special tests . . . I think I'll talk to the Interpol doctors and offer my assistance."

"Good idea Alan, keep me in the loop. Sabrina and I are flying to Zurich . . . she has some business there . . . and by the time we get there, we'll know where the funeral will be. We'll be close to Lyon if necessary. We want to pay our respects to his family."

# Vengeance - Chapter - 40

The comfortable Swiss jet touched down at the Zurich airport shortly after six in the morning after a long, but direct flight from Buenos Aires. Jake had been flying through Zurich for years and was used to the 'old' airport at Kloten. This airport, now boasted as 'Europe's finest', was a beautiful example of modern art and engineering. As Zurich was Sabrina's home town, so she too was impressed with the new airport. They were both exhausted from a combination of the situation in Buenos Aires, and the long flight.

"Do you have to go to your office right away, or should we check into a hotel . . . maybe a meal and a short nap? What do you think?" asked Jake.

Sabrina agreed. "I'm exhausted, I vote we crash for a short time, then some strong coffee and some *Gutes Schweizer Essen,* good Swiss food. It's too early to call the office, so I can do that later this morning from the hotel and tell them I'm here."

They rented a car and headed into town and checked into an upscale hotel on the Bahnhofstrasse, Zurich's banking centre. Jake always surprised himself when he checked into high priced hotels. For years of running as a poor scientist, working on a tight budget, his new found wealth gave him a whole new look at the world of travel, first class flights, first class hotels.

It was close to noon when they woke up and headed into the shower. When Sabrina called her office, she was surprised there was an important message for her. "How come? She asked Jake, "They didn't know we were going to be here."

Jake though about it, then offered "The only people who knew where we were going was Elena and Matt. It must be them, I hope everything is O.K."

"Hang on, I'll see." as she dialled the office again to get the message. It was Annette, Jacques Manet's secretary. "I'd better call her right now . . . she's probably in tears . . . and we have to find out when and where the funeral is." She stopped, as the voicemail message began to play. *"If you are calling me on this number, it means you are where I calculated you would be. Please go to Bürkliplatz at 14:00 this afternoon . . . near the flower clock."*

"What the hell is that all about?" asked Jake when Sabrina hung up.

"I have no idea . . . but there must be a reason why Annette wants to keeps this between us. Maybe the Serbian lady is listening, and she doesn't want her to know where we are."

"Well, that isn't going to work," replied Jake, "This is the only Bürkliplatz I know of, and it's well known to be in Zurich, right on the lake."

"Well, there's got to be another reason." She looked at her watch and added "We'd better get our lunch and head over there if we want to be there by 14:00."

§

It was almost right on 14:00 when the arrived at Bürkliplatz, after walking the few blocks from their hotel. A cool breeze came off the lake, refreshing in the heat of the summer, but cold this time of year. The '*Blumenuhr,* or Flower Clock' was a large garden area, shaped like a clock, with large hands turning over the flowers to tell the time. Jake looked around, the location quite familiar, although the last time he was here was on a weekend, when open-air markets were operating all along the shore, selling produce one day, and a flea market the next.

They both kept glancing around, trying to figure out why they were there. Were they supposed to meet someone, receive another message?

A short, stocky older man in a long coat was shuffling along, mumbling to himself, not paying any attention to where he was going. Jake tried to avoid the man, but he managed to bump into him quite violently.

"I beg your pardon old boy!" a familiar cockney voice came from the character that had accosted him.

Jake looked . . . stared . . . then gabbed the man by his coat collars. "Jacques! My God . . . is it you?" Sabrina let out a little scream of delight.

"Yes, my boy, it's me, in the flesh, so to speak!"

"Wha . . . what the hell is going on Jacques? We heard you were dead!"

"I am, at least as far as anyone else is concerned. Where are you staying . . . can we head out of this cold wind and enjoy a few drinks? I'll explain everything then."

So they immediately turned to head back along Bahnhofstrasse to their hotel. Both Jake and Sabrina could hardly control themselves, they had so many questions. Jacques had some difficulty convincing them to hold their questions until they were by themselves. Finally, the entered the hotel and headed into a small corner of the lounge, ordering some drinks and appies on the way. Jacques asked them again to keep their voices low, as he didn't want any of their conversation to be overheard and possibly misconstrued, as they were going to be discussing murder, sudden death, Interpol secrets and a certain Serbian madam that deals in death.

"Well," Jacques began, "I suppose I should start at the beginning."

"That's usually a good place to start." quipped Jake.

"Jake, shut up and listen!" Sabrina scolded him.

"I think because things were not going well for Madam Dejana down in Buenos Aires, and both you Jake, and I were still alive, I think she thought she had to change tactics, come out of her 'comfort zone' and do something a little more drastic. So she turned to our resident spy/translator, Malina Aleksof, and asked her, no, she actually demanded, with threats, to 'dispose of me'. This really shook up Malina, You remember last year she was supposed to do the same thing, but all that activity in Bregenz with Landau and that bunch put a stop to that."

"My God Jacques, that's terrible!"

"Was this supposed to be by poison?" asked Jake.

"Yes, she already has a small vial of poison left over from last year."

"So what did you do?" asked Sabrina.

"Well, during all this, we discovered we have a spy, a mole in Interpol somewhere, somebody who is feeding back intel directly to the Madam herself. That changed a lot of things. First, we held a very secret meeting and decided yes, I had to die!" Jacques smiled at the shocked look on the others faces. "No worries, I'm still here. To cut this short . . . we only let three people know of the plan. Besides myself, Malina, Annette and Pierre, my security/cyber guy. I hated to do it this way . . . I think it shocked a lot of people, most of my staff and many close friends . . . but it had to be realistic, authentic."

He paused, sipping on his drink. "So it all began yesterday morning, shortly after I arrived at work. Annette, my secretary, was my co-conspirator. We had managed to get a strong sedative, which was supposed to knock me out . . . so I wouldn't give it all away by doing something stupid while I was dying or 'dead'. Soooo . . . . it was quite dramatic! I dropped a few files on the floor and laid down, while Annette yelled bloody murder and then called 112 . . . the emergency number and got an ambulance there within minutes. Much to everyone's horror and surprise, I was loaded onto a trolley, and packed off in the ambulance." Jacques paused here, glancing at all of them with a mischievous look on his face. "We had to not only make it look good, we wanted as many people as possible to see it happening."

"So, did they take you to the hospital? What next?"

"Yes, off to the hospital, but only as far as the entrance to the emergency department. From there, they loaded a body on a trolley from the ambulance, and wheeled him into the hospital."

"But, that wasn't you?"

"No, I had it arranged beforehand for them to have a body in the ambulance . . . some poor chap who died from an overdose the night before."

"My God, Jacques," cried Sabrina "All this charade was to convince anyone watching that it was you?"

"Yes, we knew the only way it would work was to have my dead body show up at the hospital. It just so happened he also had papers on him declaring that he was M. Jacques Manet, of Interpol. In the meantime, I managed to slip out and take a rental car I had planted in the hospital parking lot . . . and *Voila!*, here I am!"

"Wow!" said Jake, "All that must have taken a little planning . . . and precision."

"Actually, no. Annette and I worked out most of it the night before. We wanted to keep it simple, few people involved. So, by now, our lady in Beograd will be very happy! One of her arch-enemies is dead!"

"I've never had drinks with a dead man before," said Jake, smiling as he raised his glass. "How do I do this. . .wish you health and a long life? Doesn't seem quite right!"

# Vengeance - Chapter - 41

The three conspirators spent the next few hours in the bar, trying to figure out what comes next. Jacques was laughing, mainly at himself. "Well!" he said in a low whisper, "We managed to kill me and dispose of the body, almost, and now we have to figure out the next step. Sorry guys, we didn't carry through with the planning of this little exercise. We just wanted to take some pressure off of Malina . . . and maybe throw Dejana off balance."

Sabrina had be quiet up to that point, but answered "Considering the situation Jacques, I think you've planned and 'executed' your death quite well. I'm sure all hell has broken loose back at Interpol, and I am also sure that your 'mole' or 'spy' has dutifully reported back to Dr. Babić. We now have to figure out what her next move might be." She paused, looking at the men. "I'm pretty sure she is going to attend your funeral . . . whenever that is. She knows that Jake will be there for sure, along with many other enemies she has made in recent years. I don't think she'll miss the chance to see you all in one place."

"Christ! I hadn't thought of that!" said Jake, almost choking on his drink. "And what a chance she would have to dispose of us all, in one fell swoop, so to speak!"

Jacques was shaking his head. "Good Grief! You don't think she would try something like that, do you?"

"Don't under-estimate her guys" advised Sabrina . . . "I'm sure she is capable of anything like that! First, Jacques . . . have you decided when you'll have your funeral?"

That brought more laughs, and they decided they had to change the subject, at least temporarily and have something to eat.

Before the moved into the dining room for dinner, Jacques pulled out a phone. Before anyone could jump on him, he told them "No, No, this is a special phone that my cyber guy, Pierre, gave to me before I left. I must only use this phone . . . my own phone and my ID is still on my 'body', which will end up on Annette's desk before long. I want to catch him before he leaves the office.

"Hello, Bonjour Pierre? . . . yes everything is going as planned, please thank Annette for all her help, I couldn't have died without her." he started to laugh. "If this wasn't such a serious subject, it would be funny." Jacques paused, listening to Pierre. "O.K. Pierre, I don't want to get into that now, I'll call you again soon, we have a few plans to make. Please ask Annette to go ahead and plan my funeral, ask her to invite Bert Jackson from the F.B.I., and Scott Anderson from W.C.B.. She can let me know the usual way, on that special number. I'll call her in a day or so." He listened again then added "Yes, both Jake and Sabrina are here with me . . .we'll let you know."

As he hung up his phone, Jake and Sabrina waited for some news. "Well . . . what's happening back home? Did they buy it?"

"Yes . . . everyone is devastated with my death, nice to know really. Apparently, I died on the way to the hospital, so I was not even admitted . . . that was so nobody could come to visit me. Annette and Pierre went to collect my personal things and my body was delivered to a *mortuaire*. Annette will set things up and let us know when the funeral is. I suppose it will be in Lyon, there is no reason why not."

"I must call Alan Cook, back at the office . . . I want him here to give us some expertise on poisons, and what we might expect. Maybe I'll bring my entire crew over to Lyon, they should all attend the funeral. So, where did you stay last night Jacques? asked Jake.

"I drove directly to a cousin I have just outside of town, I hadn't made any plans. I have a rental car . . . from Lyon . . . I left my car in my usual parking spot at Interpol. As far as anyone else is concerned, I do not exist here."

"Good!" answered Jake, "I think you should check in here, in this hotel . . . in fact I'll get another room for you, they know me here . . . so your name doesn't show up anywhere."

"This place is a little rich for me Jake."

"Don't worry, I'll deal with that, it's the least I can do for an old friend who has just died." he said, laughing.

"O.K. guys" interrupted Sabrina, "Here's the plan . . . we meet for breakfast tomorrow morning, after which, we have to go shopping for you Jacques, get you some fresh clothes . . . we don't know how long we'll be here. Then we have to meet again, develop a plan . . . not only to protect ourselves from the Serbian Bitch, but to figure out a way we can catch her doing something. . . something we can actually pin on her!"

§

Dejana was excited. She had just heard from her spy at Interpol that her enemy, Jacques Manet had just collapsed at work and was taken to the hospital, arriving dead. She then checked with Malina, who confirmed, in tears, that Jacques was in fact dead. At that point, nobody knew when the funeral would be, but Dejana knew she had to attend. She knew that Jake Prescott and maybe his smart little girlfriend would probably attend. Maybe even some of the other law enforcement nuisances might be there. She shivered with excitement as she considered all the opportunities this might present. Opportunities to get even, to seek revenge for herself, and to avenge all the lovers she had lost because of these people. As she considered all this, she realized she was violating the main rule she had tried to enforce with her employees. "Don't let personal feelings or grievances cloud your judgement or get in the way of your job." She couldn't help it . . . this was too great of an opportunity to miss. Now . . . how was she going to do it?

§

Back in Buenos Aires, Mateo Perez had his hands full. Both he and Elena were devastated with the news of Jacques Manet's death, and they too suspected that the Serbian doctor had a hand in it. In the meantime, all Hell had broken loose with the drug gangs, combined with the MS13 street gang influx. His street level informer, Joaquin Garcia had given him some warning, but there was nothing he could do about it. Joaquin had told him that the Serbs were pushing for dominance over the drug traffic, both in and out of the territory. Because hundreds of millions, even billions of dollars were involved, Matt felt completely useless and ineffective, and could do nothing about it. He wanted to talk to Jake and Sabrina to find out more about Jacques' death, but he hadn't been able to call them once since it happened.

Then Annette, Jacques' secretary in Lyon, called him and let him know what was happening. He couldn't believe the news and was quick to call Elena and swear her to secrecy as well.

"Pack your bags my Love, we're heading off to Lyon, France. To Hell with all these gangs down here, this is something I have to do!"

# Vengeance - Chapter - 42

Dejana had finally come to a conclusion. She called in one of her top poison experts for a meeting. Although Dejana was an expert in plants, botanical and other 'natural' toxins, she respected Ivan Petrov's expertise in the modern poisons, the nerve agents and binary chemical weapons. Petrov was Russian, and used to work at the Soviet Chemical Research Institute, *GosNIIOKhT*, a secret organization responsible for the production of many nerve agents, including *Novichok*. Novichok agents became to public attention after they were used to poison opponents of the Russian government. The most recent case was Alexei Navalny in 2020, which was still playing out in the press years later.

Ivan had joined Dejana's group shorty after 2019, when the Organization for the Prohibition of Chemical Weapons (OPCW) added Novichok to the 'list of controlled substance'. Dejana was quick to offer Ivan a job, as she felt this kind of expertise would help her organization.

She explained the situation to Ivan, laying out all her wishes and problems that she saw. "There is going to be a few people there, I don't anticipate too many, but it would be nice if I could somehow target just a few . . . the ones I want."

Ivan grasped the problem right away. "So, all of his friends will be there . . . the ones you want to target?"

"Yes, I think so. They will be involved somehow, I'm sure."

"I would imagine they will be the pallbearers, don't you think?" he asked.

"Yes, I would think so." Dejana said, her mind whirling. "Do you think... do you have a poison that works on contact... if somebody touches it?"

"Yes, of course, one of the nerve agents could work. *Tabun, Soman* or *VX* is a possibility, but our old friend *Novichok* is about ten times more lethal. For touching, I can make a newer version, better for skin absorption."

"Good!" Dejana exclaimed... she could hardly control her excitement as she rubbed her hand on his butt. "You go ahead and make some, I'll figure out a way how to deliver it."

She had already figured a way to deliver the agent. The pallbearers have to lift the casket, and carry it to the grave. Each of the people she wanted to eliminate would be handling the casket. "How appropriate," she thought, as she considered the results of her plans. "I just have to find out who is handling the funeral, and when.

§

Annette was busy in Lyon, deciding those details. She found it weird, humorous and quite exciting to arrange a funeral for her boss, who she had helped to 'die', and was not really dead. She was so glad all their quickly made plans worked out as well as they did. But she felt bad that all their colleagues in the office were so broke up about Jacques' death, and she couldn't tell them otherwise. She received a call from Jake Prescott earlier in the day, letting her know how everyone was, and how her dead person was faring. They both managed to talk in code, just in case somebody had access to their call. She told Jake that she had called Bert Jackson at the F.B.I., and Scott Anderson at W.C.B., swearing them both to secrecy. She was surprised they already had heard of Jacques' death, and were relieved to hear he was still alive, and were both willing to go along with the game and help anyway they could. She asked both to be pallbearers. She now had six pallbearers, Bert Jackson, Scott Anderson, Jake Prescott, Alan Cook, Mateo Perez, and Pierre Dupuis and from their office. Quite an international group, she thought, laughing to herself, very appropriate for such an important man. Now all she had to do was set a date.

§

Jake, Sabrina and Jacques were having fun, just being together and being able to talk, without the threat of somebody trying to kill them. Jacques was thrilled to be able to talk to Sabrina, his 'wonder woman' he had admired for so long, but had not spent any time with. After the first day, Alan Cook joined them with the rest of Jake's office crew from Vancouver. Although Alan was a little 'jet-lagged', he added to the fun, being able to compare notes about places in England they both knew well. It was also the first time Jake had met some of Sabrina's colleagues in the F.I.S., and they were equally fascinated by the little deception they were playing.

Sabrina told Jake later "O.K., my guys from F.I.S. are loaning us a surveillance van, they are going to work with Interpol, and monitor everyone at the funeral . . . you know . . . scan faces, photographs, the whole thing! We want to know everyone there, and we want to be able to watch their every move. God, Jake, I'm worried, we have no idea what she might do."

"Don't worry, my love, Jacques doesn't want to die twice in one week. He's asked your guys to supply the communications stuff as well. We'll all be wired up, mikes, earwigs, the whole nine yards.

O.K., just so you know, everyone is going to stay at the International Hotel, just down the street from Interpol. It is big enough we can lose Jacques in there and keep him anonymous, plus it is very close to Interpol. Annette has set up the funeral for next Wednesday, so everyone should have arrived, even our unwanted guests.

§

Malina tried again . . .damn! It spilled again! Each evening, she practiced her slight of hand, but was failing miserably. She was trying to pour a small vial of poison into a cup of coffee or a drink, without being obvious about it. She had a small bottle, the same size as the fatal dose Dejana had given her, that she had been saving for over a year. She tried slipping it under her watch strap . . . that didn't work. Then she attached it to her wrist with an elastic band. At the correct moment, she would superstitiously pull the cork out, and try to empty the vial into another glass without it being obvious. She knew if she practiced it enough, she would master it . . . it was so important! She then practiced the motion while reaching over to move the glass . . . as if she was trying to relocate it to a safer place. That worked better, and by the end of the evening, she was getting to be an expert. All it took was something else to distract the person's attention for a few seconds. She only hoped she could pull it off.

# Vengeance - Chapter - 43

### Lyon, France

Pierre Dupuis had been busy since Jacques' 'death'. As he worked with Annette on the details, things were progressing well. He still hadn't found out who the internal spy was, but he felt he was getting closer. He suspected one of his own crew . . . a young computer 'nerd' who had access to much of what was going on. Setting up little 'traps' was his specialty as a cyber crime expert, and he knew he was good at it. It became a challenge, trying to lure his prey to fall for 'low hanging fruit', without making it too obvious. Not only did he have to trap the individual, but to do it in such a way that they could charge him with the crime and put him out of business. He definitely wanted to do this before the funeral, just in case further action was planned by Dejana.

After an entire day of concentrated effort, Pierre narrowed it down to a young woman on the same floor as Jacques Manet. That was how she kept track of Jacques' movements, when he came and went in the office, as well as further information on his phone calls. Pierre realized that computer knowledge and abilities were not only a male skill, but he was always amazed at the high level of skills and finesse achieved by the women. This one was certainly a challenge. Quietly, he arranged for an arrest team to show up one morning, seize her and her computer, and as much other evidence as possible.

That problem solved, at least for now, he concentrated on helping Annette with the funeral arrangements. They had decided on a day, and the format of the service. It would be a brief graveside service, after the casket was delivered and carried by six pallbearers to the grave. Both he and Annette had talked with all of the candidates for pallbearers, and they knew what was expected of them. He would be monitoring the proceedings via video surveillance from the van supplied by F.I.S., together with Sabrina and Jacques Manet. Jacques was still laughing over the fact that he would be watching his own funeral on T.V. They would set up multiple cameras around the site, and record everything. All of the images were being processed with facial recognition software to try to determine who attended. They were looking in particular for Dr. Dejana Babić. Sabrina brought up the curious fact that nobody . . . none of their crowd had actually seen Dejana, so they had no idea what she looked like. The Interpol software however, did know what she looked like . . . from both Serbian passport information and other official documents. Security had been increased at the airport and all train stations and the software was getting a workout. They wanted to know the minute she arrived in Lyon . . . or anywhere in France!

The surveillance paid off . . . She was detected arriving at the Lyon-Saint Exupéry Airport on a flight from Beograd, Serbia, on the Monday, two days before the funeral. They all were glad Dejana's spy had let her know the date, otherwise she might have missed the funeral and all their plans would be in vain. Jacques was not satisfied, he wanted everyone on every flight from Serbia checked out. This precaution also paid off, as a person arriving on the same plane as Dejana rang a few bells. He was a Russian by the name of Ivan Petrov, Interpol had a sizable file on this guy, as he was a Russian poison expert who used to work at the Soviet Chemical Research Institute, GosNIIOKhT. Jacques was pleased with his decision to check others flying in . . . especially anybody who might have a connection with poisons in any way.

Sabrina was also interested, studying his Interpol file as well as everything F.I.S. had on him. She had joined the others in the surveillance van, now set up close to the graveyard as a control centre, monitoring communication between individuals and headquarters. "My God, Jacques . . .look at this . . . this guy was involved with *Novichok* . . .that's the stuff that killed those people in England a few years ago, and almost killed that Russian protester."

Jacques looked over the information. His brow creased with worry as he turned to Sabrina. "Oh my dear, this could be worse than we expected, if this guy has some *Novichok*, or his latest version of it . . . God knows what they might try."

"What's up guys?" Jake asked, as he entered the van. "You look pretty serious."

"Jake, glad you're here, look at this." She pulled all the info about Petrov up on the screen. Jake's face took on a grim appearance as he read the information.

"*Novichok!* Shit!" he exclaimed! Get Alan Cook in here . . . he knows a lot about that as he followed that fiasco in England. I think he knew some of the guys that worked on it, he might be able to tell us something."

§

At that moment, Dejana was having a meeting with Ivan Petrov. "So . . . have you figured out a way to deliver the goods to my victims?" She asked.

"Yes my dear, I think we have a perfect way to target your people exclusively and very specifically."

"Excellent!" cried Dejana. "Please explain to me how this is going to take place."

"Well, first, as we all assemble around the gravesite, the hearse arrives from *la chambre mortuaire,* the casket will be wheeled out of the rear door, onto a portable stand. The six pallbearers will gather around the casket, each one grasping a handle." Ivan said with a sneer . . . "At that point . . . their fate is sealed."

Dejana stared, "Wha . . . oh! How clever!" She exclaimed. "You mean the handles?"

"Yes, my dear . . . the handles . . . once they grasp the handles . . . all is lost for that individual."

"Magnificent!" screamed Dejana, "Perfect! Just what I wanted . . . and how long will it take?"

"Well with normal Novichok, it could take a few days, but with my 'new and improved version', they should experience symptoms almost immediately. Death will follow shortly after . . . and there is not much they can do about it."

# Vengeance - Chapter - 44

Malina was nervous. The entire 'Manet's death' deception was wearing on her nerves. She was glad that Pierre had caught the 'spy' in the building, but she had to be careful who she talked to and what she said. She was one of the few that knew that Jacques Manet was still alive and they were setting a trap for Dejana. Malina had decided that even if Interpol and all their associates could not stop Dejana, it was up to her to do it. She was tired of Dejana's constant pressure, constant threats to her family and inferred threats to herself. She had no qualms about turning the tables on her. Too many people had died at her hands, or by somebody else's hands under her direction. She still had her little vial of poison, and she was becoming expert at delivering it into a drink very surreptitiously. She just had to set up the opportunity to do it.

The opportunity came later that evening when Dejana called her at home. They talked for a short time, mainly about Jacques' funeral, over which Malina acted devastated and eventually broke into tears. She had been practicing that as well, and was convinced she did a good job. They agreed to meet shortly after the funeral for a drink, as Dejana had some bonus money to give to Malina, bonus money for disposing of Jacques Manet, which Malina thought rather humorous. She told Dejana where the funeral was and she suggested a small bistro nearby to have a drink. Malina was familiar with the area more than Dejana, so she picked a spot she knew, a place where she felt comfortable she could complete her 'duty'.

Dejana asked Malina if she knew what happened to her 'spy' at Interpol. Malina pleaded ignorance, as if she was not aware of the other woman's operation, before or after Pierre caught her, and she certainly didn't want Dejana to know she was involved in any way. "I don't know . . . that guy is always running security checks . . . making sure we don't get hacked . . . you know."

§

Bert Jackson and Scott Anderson arrived together at Lyon-Saint Exupéry airport, and shared a taxi into town. Neither of them knew of the deception until they arrived at the hotel and were greeted by Jake. "As soon as you guys check in, meet me in the lounge . . . way down in the back corner."

"Sounds good Jake, I could use a drink, then a few hours sleep."

"The sleep might have to wait, once you learn what I have to tell you."

Before long, they joined Jake and the rest of the gang in the bar. Things were as expected, the usual greetings all around, until Jacques stood up and greeted the two. Two shocked looks, two open mouths. "What the hell? Both men stuttered. Joyous greetings and hugs all around! "Oh boy . . . you definitely owe us a drink, Manet!" It was a boisterous time for all of them to get together once again. "We haven't done this since last year." Jake observed. "Maybe we should make it an annual thing?"

"Right!" answered Scott. "Maybe when things calm down? You know, when the Serbian threat is neutralized?"

"Good idea" added Bert Jackson, "From what I've learned so far Jake, this might be the time . . . the time we catch this bitch?"

"Well, we hope so. Everything is set up to lure her here. It depends on whether she takes the bait."

"You mean of course, that we are the bait?"

"Yes, at least that's what Jacques had in mind when he 'died' for this whole sting operation. What better time is she going to catch almost all of her enemies together in one spot?"

Bert Jackson interrupted with "What about this Russian guy . . . the poison expert . . . I only heard about him recently . . . don't have a lot of intel on him."

"Alan, could you fill in Bert on this guy?" asked Jake. "Bert, this is Alan Cook, my chemical expert from Vancouver."

Alan acknowledged Bert, as he had only heard of him from reports, never in person. "Well Bert, I'm sure you've heard about the Novichok poisonings in England last year, as well as the more recent attacks on Navalny, the Russian protester? Well, this guy that just arrived here with Dr. Babić, Ivan Petrov, worked at the same Soviet centre that developed Novichok. He quit there when things became 'difficult' and joined Dr. Babić, so it's a good guess that he's up to his old tricks."

"God! I can understand why you guys are worried. I hope you've got a lot of antidote on hand?" said Bert.

Alan coughed a little with a smile and said soberly "That's the point Bert . . . there is no 'antidote' for this stuff! Especially if this Ivan Petrov has been busy in Babić's lab in Serbia. Who knows what he's come up with this time?"

"Holeee . . . I hope at least he's under surveillance." Bert exclaimed.

"Oh yes! You'll learn all the details tomorrow. Annette is setting up a meeting for all of us to attend.

The rest of the evening was devoted to catching up with each other's lives. Most of the questions were directed to Jake and Sabrina, as most of them had not been exposed to Sabrina's charms before. Jake started to feel a little jealous, as he was losing control of his girl friend. Jacques was throughly enjoying the entire scene, being the 'main character' in this play.

"Relax Jake," he teased Jake, "Sabrina is still yours, you don't have anything to worry about. This is just a break for these guys, and Sabrina is just 'icing on the cake", so to speak. I think the funniest thing about this entire scene is that Sabrina could hold her own with any of these guys, whether it's in an intensive computer investigation, on the shooting range, or in a knock-down drag out confrontation." He laughed and added "We saw that in Bregenz last year, didn't we?"

"Yes we did, Jacques." replied Jake, already feeling better. "Let's see if we can get some dinner delivered to this room. I'm sure everyone is ready for something!"

# Vengeance - Chapter - 45

Annette called Jake at the hotel and asked Jake to schedule a meeting with everyone to discuss their plans for the funeral. They met in a private meeting room at the hotel later that day. In addition to Jacques' friends and colleagues in Lyon, Jake's Vancouver staff, Alan Cook, Peter Wong and Shannon Hall had flown in for the funeral. Jake was surprised at the number of people there, as they were trying to keep the group who knew about Jacques' deception as small as possible. For safety reason, and constant coaxing by Alan Cook, the local Sûreté had been invited.

Alan started the meeting with a brief explanation of what he was afraid of. "Folks, from what I have been told, our 'Mistress of Murder' in Serbia has a new partner . . . Ivan Petrov, whose expertise is nerve agents and binary chemical weapons. Apparently, his specialty is Novichok, which I'm sure you have all heard of."

Murmurs went through the group, both to acknowledge the Novichok information, but also a chuckle for Alan's new designation of the 'Serbian Bitch', calling her the 'Mistress of Murder'.

Alan continued "Whatever you have heard about Novichok . . . it is worse! I have not had direct experience with this material, but I have been very close to someone who has.

My colleague and good friend was involved in the investigation of the incident in Amesbury, U.K. a few years ago, where the Skripal family and two others were poisoned. This guy that just arrived in Lyon, worked for the Russians in that secret lab developing these monsters. If he is the expert I think he might be, he could have been working for the Serbian gal for some time to develop a newer, deadlier version." He paused a moment, then looked out over the group. "As you can see . . . we have several new additions to our gang. This might be due to my fears and constant warnings I have been voicing ever since I arrived. Hopefully, I'm all wrong and prove to be an over-anxious alarmist. I hope so. For your information, here's what we have planned so far, and here's how all these people fit in. I've been working with Jacques' secretary, Annette, so I'll let her take over and give you some details."

Annette stood and addressed the group. *"Bonjour mes amis! Bienvenue!* And for those who have come from afar . . . Hello my friends, welcome to Lyon! Thanks Alan, for your grim and sobering comments about Novichok. Let's hope we don't have to deal with that monster. But . . . just in case . . . Pierre and I have been working on this, with rather mixed feelings I might add." as she glanced over with a smile to Jacques. "The funeral will be held at 12:00 on Wednesday, at the Loyasse Cemetery, the *Cimetiére de Loyasse.* This cemetery is on the west side of town, in the F*ifth Arondissement,* not far from here. The Sûreté has joined us, after all, this is their jurisdiction, with a couple of hazmat teams. I have asked for this, just in case we have a situation where what Alan calls 'bits and pieces' of Novichok flying around. When we checked with law enforcement in England, they said things became very complicated when they discovered that everything they touched was contaminated from someone touching something then touching something else. I case the same thing happens here . . .we're not taking any chances . . . the haz-mat teams will move in and take over."

The man in charge of the Sûreté spoke up and added "We understand the need for this to be a discreet operation. To begin with, no overpowering police force visible, so our team will be standing ready, tucked away behind one of the many buildings at the cemetery site."

Sabrina stood and spoke up. This is Andre Kohl, my colleague fro the F.I.S., who has volunteered to provide our communications throughout the operation. The reason he is here to help is that all of you have your normal jobs to deal with, and this is sort of an *ad hoc* operation, which might or might not be successful." She looked over the room, acknowledging Scott Hamilton from the TV network WBC, and Bert Jackson from the FBI, who had both joined them that morning. "There are those here who have been working for years to bring this lady down. Maybe we can do something on Wednesday. She turned again towards Scott Anderson and added "Scott, it seems very time we see you, it's to cover some disaster. Maybe this time, you can write the closing chapter." She paused and turned back to the group. "I'm going to turn things over to Andre now, to explain the communications portion."

"Hi folks . . . I'm really impressed with the international representation we have here today. I shouldn't be surprised however, as Jacques was a respected Interpol officer . . .sorry . . . I shouldn't have said 'was', as he still is a respected Interpol officer."

"Jolly good, Andre! Yes, I'm still here." As everyone laughed.

Andre continued. "We will supply several of you with two-way radio links, so we can talk to each other, in case something has to be relayed. For the six pall-bearers, they will also have two way communications, a small earwig device in their ear, so we can talk to them as required. Considering the need for discretion, I'd rather not have all the pall-bearers talking to us or to one one another. Better they just listen, unless something unusual happens. I will be on this end of the conversation, Annette and Jacques will be monitoring the video cameras, and letting me know what's happening."

Annette stood again. "Thanks Andre, we appreciate the help from F.I.S. on this. So, the six pall-bearers, you'll all be wearing dark suits, white shirts, and . . . " as she turned with a bag from a men's wear store. "Here are your ties. A light blue . . . so your outfits will almost match the Interpol flag or crest. That's my nod to the fashion industry, after all, he was an important man in the organization." She smiled . . . "Sorry Jacques . . . I slipped into the past tense as well." She stopped then pulled out another bag, and pulled out some nitrile gloves, as well as several pairs of white cotton gloves. "Each of the pall-bearers will wear these. I was going to suggest only the cotton gloves, but Alan insisted they wear the nitrile gloves under those gloves."

Alan stood again to reinforce Annette's warnings. "This is to protect you just in case you touch something contaminated. These cotton gloves are just for show, they do nothing to protect you."

An officer from the Sûreté then rose. *"Bonjour,* the only vehicle you will see is the hearse when it arrives with Jacques." He smiled over at Jacques. "Our observation and communications van will be tucked over behind one of those large monuments, near Jacques' gravesite. We have already installed several video cameras around the site, so we can observe and record all the people attending the funeral. All of the video capture will be forwarded and processed by Interpol's facial recognition software, we want to know who is here, and be able to keep track of them throughout the service.

# Vengeance - Chapter - 46

The day began cool but clear. "Not typical funeral weather" thought Annette, who had a vision of fog, rain and miserable weather for a funeral. At least that's what she always saw on television. She arrived early, together with Pierre and his support staff to make sure things were set up in preparation of the events to follow. They met in the surveillance van set up amongst some large monuments behind one of the buildings on site From there, they couldn't see the actual gravesite, but once the system was 'turned on', they had ample views of the entire area, especially where most of the guests would be standing. It was these 'guests' that they were most interested in . . . one or two in particular.

Sabrina and Jake had also arrived, both interested in how this operation was going to proceed. Annette opened her bag of goodies and took out six pairs of white cotton gloves and six pairs of nitrile gloves, all in large size for the men who would be wearing them. She had already delivered some blue ties to the men, so they could arrive in full 'dress uniform'. She turned to Jake and gave him a final inspection. "Looking good Jake . . . don't you think so, Sabrina?"

"I always think so," replied Sabrina with a smile, "But yes, all my 'men' will look really sharp today."

Before long, Mateo and Eleni arrived, and Scott Anderson and Bert Jackson shortly after. Annette immediately pulled all the men aside for a little pep talk and last minute instructions. "O.K. guys, here's our schedule for today. The service will be in just over an hour, so you can't stay here until then. We don't know when our 'guests' will arrive, so we don't want you guys arriving suspiciously together from behind this building. In fact, it would be better if you arrived together in a taxi, like you all just came from the hotel."

"Good idea Annette," answered Bert, "We can do that now . . . we'll see you in about twenty minutes?"

"Good! . . . then Jacques will arrive in the hearse in about thirty minutes, and things will get started about then."

Jacques had been observing this and couldn't help but laugh at the ridiculous situation he was witnessing. Annette looked at him crossly and said "And you M. Manet . . . can make yourself scarce and make sure nobody outside of this van spots you! You're supposed to be in the casket!" she said with a laugh.

"You'll be on the communications desk with Pierre, so you should not move from there during the entire procedure."

"O.K. everyone!" Pierre announced. "I hope you all keep your wits sharp and your eyes wide open. Face recognition is one thing, but only your eyes and brain, together with years of observation and surveillance experience can spot a suspicious activity, a person 'out of place', or an action that 'doesn't seem quite right'. These are the things we want to watch for. For the pallbearers, this task will be a little more difficult as you have another duty to perform. You won't have multiple screens to watch, only your surroundings. Not only that . . . you've been asked to keep communications at a minimum . . . only if necessary."

Jacques interrupted at this point to say "O.K. chaps, this is it . . . possibly our best chance to catch our elusive lady from Serbia, and actually have something to pin on her. But, remember this . . . she is very clever . . . so we do not know what she might try . . . or who is helping her. So keep your wits about you . . . watch everyone . . . if somebody doesn't look right, or somebody is out of place . . . that might be all we can go on! Good luck . . . *Bon chance!*"

The site cleared off, leaving only a few people in charge of the service. A few guests had arrived, mostly Interpol staff and colleagues who either worked with Jacques, or just knew him. The six pallbearers arrived in a taxi, all looking very sober and serious, taking up positions on opposite sides of the area where the hearse would arrive.

Annette, Eleni and Sabrina were watching for inside the van. "Damn, they look good!" don't they? said Sabrina, which bought laughs from the other two women, along with comments of agreement.

"Keep your mind on the task at hand, ladies," joked Pierre. He was in the middle of a communications check with his computer department, making sure all of the camera images were being forwarded and scanned for recognition. Pierre scanned the images himself, but was at a disadvantage as he did not know who he was looking for. Large prints of passport photos of both Dejana and Ivan were posted up on the wall of the van, just to keep their images in mind as they scanned their surroundings on the computers.

The hearse arrived on time, and pulled into the area just in front of the six pallbearers. Before the driver got out, another man jumped out of the rear of the hearse. Dressed in black, he looked like most of the personnel from the *mortuaire*. He looked around, reached inside and pulled out a small cart and set it up just outside of the rear of the hearse, with the cart's top level with the rear of the hearse. He then walked away just as the driver exited the vehicle. The driver came around and reached into the hearse and pulled out the casket onto the cart that the other man had just set up. He then backed off, and nodded to the six men standing by and stood at attention beside the van.

That was the pallbearers' cue to advance and pick up the casket, which they did, each man grasping a handle of the casket and lifting it off the cart. Jake had a small problem as he did not want to surrender his cane, just in case his leg gave out at the wrong time, but he worked it out with one hand for the casket and one for the cane.

Sabrina was watching this from inside the surveillance van. Something was different from their practice run. Who was that guy that set up the cart? The *mortuaire* told them that the driver would be doing that . . . and where is he now?

Alan cook screamed over her shoulder "The handles . . . the handles . . .that's how they're doing it?"

Sabrina immediately yelled over the comm link "Stop you guys! *Arrêtez, ne bougez pas!* Don't move! *Ne toucher à rien avec vos gants!* Don't touch anything with your gloves!"

Andre Kohl, the F.I.S. communications guy joined the plea with "Stop . . . lower the casket to the ground, and raise your hands up without touching anything.

Almost as if on cue, the hearse driver staggered from his position beside the hearse and collapsed in front of the others. All fearful of doing the wrong thing, all six pallbearers stood at attention, hands raised. "What the hell?" was the collective question.

Within seconds, two men, fully dressed in hazmat protective gear arrived from behind the building where they had been stationed. They immediately placed the downed driver on to a stretcher and carried him off. Two more hazmat suits arrived and with a practiced skill, proceeded to remove the gloves from the six men, carefully sealing them in plastic bags and taking them away. They scanned the men with some optical scanners, looking for residual bits of the offending material. They all had visions of having to strip off their clothes and be hosed down or showered with some disinfectant or some other nasty stuff.

Annette looked over to Pierre . . . "what the hell, Pierre . . . how did we miss that? Where did that other guy come from . . . and where did he go?"

Jacques was on the phone to his people. Has anyone spotted her . . . or that Ivan guy? He asked, hoping that somebody, somewhere had spotted their quarry. The answer came back right away. "Yes, M. Manet, we have one sighting of her on the edge of the group of guests on the west side, but she disappeared as soon as the hazmat guys showed up. I suppose she figured it was all over, her little trick did not work."

"Is anyone tracking her now?" asked Jacques, knowing that it was unlikely and that would be the last they would see of her.

"No" . . . was the answer he expected

"Too bloody close for my thoughts," said Alan . . . "That could have been so bad . . . she could have wiped out all her enemies at once, just by picking up that damned casket! I'm so glad I insisted on nitrile gloves under those cotton ones."

Jacques was not giving up. "How about Ivan . . . did we see him . . . and how about that guy in the hearse. . . where is he?"

Jacques was frustrated beyond belief. How can three fugitives escape from a surveillance operation so easily? The place was surrounded by video cameras. Pierre tried to calm Jacques down, "We'll find them, we probably have them on video, but it will take us a short time to view a lot of it, but we'll get them."

## Vengeance - Chapter - 47

Dejana was furious once again. How did they know . . . how did they prepare for what she thought was a perfect plan? It was so close, she thought, so close to eliminating all three of the people she hated the most, with three more just as a bonus! She had spotted several of the video cameras set up around the funeral site. Something she had expected, but did not want to stick around to deal with the interrogations that would surely follow. She had a half hour before she was expected for lunch with Malina. Referring to the city map in her hands, she finally figured out where Malina's little bistro was.

When she arrived at the designated spot, Malina was already seated, ready to order a drink. She grabbed the waiter and ordered two glasses of Raki. The waiter answered something that Dejana couldn't understand. Malina interrupted, explaining what the waiter had said. "They don't have Raki, but they do have either *Pastis*, or *Cognac*."

Dejana recognized 'Cognac', and ordered two glasses for them. She was impatient and irritable, and when the drink finally arrived, she was pleased it was in a large brandy snifter. Without a moment to lose, she gulped the entire glass down, and was calling the waiter for another. Malina couldn't believe her luck, as she watched Dejana, she knew her wits were not as sharp as usual. That, plus the fact that the Cognac was served in a wide-mouthed snifter, a much easier target to drop something into.

Malina rose up and reaching over, passed her glass to Dejana. "Oh my, I hate to see you so upset . . . here, take mine, I can wait for him to bring another." She said softly, her slight of hand working flawlessly over the large mouth snifter.

"Malina . . . why are you wearing those gloves?" Dejana asked.

"Oh!, I forgot I even had them on. Annette asked all of us to wear them today . . . I suppose it had something to do with what they were expecting."

Dejana thought about this and realized they were prepared for Ivan's attack . . . but how?

The waiter soon brought another glass, which Malina took politely and started to sip the golden liquor. Dejana did not wait, she gulped down the second glass, and pulled out some money to hand to Malina. "Thank you Malina. You did a good job . . . it's too bad they figured out our little operation today." Malina thanked her for the money, knowing she had earned it, one way or another. She watched Dejana, as her face started to turn red, her eyes grew large, and her voice began to falter. "Wha . . . what is . . . ?" Suddenly, understanding dawned on her. "Malina . . . wha . . . why?"

Malina suddenly became emboldened, knowing this monster was finally breathing her last . . . through a poison of her own making. Malina couldn't remember if it was the one that effected the heart, the brain, the nervous system, or what, but Malina was certain Dejana did not have long to live. Dejana's breathing was ragged, her eyes wide, she clutched at her chest, vainly trying to remove the weights that were crushing her. Realization finally dawned on her what was happening.

Malina stood up, leaning over closer to her enemy's face. Wanting to take advantage of the situation as much as possible she said very slowly and clearly. "And just so you know, Jacques

Manet is still alive and well, this entire funeral thing was staged just to bring you and your Russian buddy to Lyon! And it worked!"

Dejana's last breaths escaped her lips as her mouth twisted in a grimace of hate . Malina did not waste time. She placed some money on the table, pulled her scarf closer around her face, and quickly walked away, disappearing into the complex neighbourhoods of western Lyon. Before long, she pulled off her head scarf and Annette's nitrile gloves and quickly dropped them into a street trash can . . . she felt strangely good!

§

They all met later that afternoon at the hotel, analyzing the operation and comparing notes. Jacques thanked all of them for attending his funeral, announcing the next round of drinks was on him!

"Did they ever track that Russian . . . Ivan?" someone asked.

"No, but they'll get him when he tries to leave the country."

"Don't count on it," Jacques said. "He is in Europe and he can travel all over, unimpeded, no passports, no border checks. They probably won't catch him until he tries to fly out of any airport."

"So what about Dejan Babić? We never did catch her on the video recordings."

"Yes we did," answered Pierre and Andre together. Andre continued "She was spotted on the periphery of the crowd, and then again when she left shortly after the casket thing. I assume she did not want to see the results of that sting."

"So . . . she got away?"

"Well . . . yes and no . . . she got away from us, but not her fate."

"What do you mean?" someone asked.

"She was found dead at the table of a little bistro on the west end of town . . . not far from the cemetery. It was less than an hour after the funeral. The police questioned the waiter, and he couldn't remember much, he thought there was another lady there, but she left earlier. Apparently, Dr. Babić downed almost three large glasses of brandy, so it appeared she was stressed out about something. The only prints they could find on the glasses were the waiter's and Dejana's. It will take an autopsy to discover what killed her . . . but I suspect it was some of her own poison."

"Maybe she was realizing we were closing in on her and decided to end it all."

"I doubt it." someone offered.

Jacques glanced over to Malina, who was sitting by herself, very quiet. Their eyes met, and a message of understanding traveled between them. Jacques smiled grimly as he thought about what that girl must have suffered to be able to do this terrible deed.

Their meeting continued, as they listened to reports by Pierre's cyber team, results of the Sûreté investigation at the cafe, chemical analysis findings by the Hazmat team, and finally, an update on the hearse driver's condition, which was not good. When questioned by the police, he said that the extra man told him he was sent for added security and to assist. Apparently, the driver had contacted the handles of the casket with only thin driving gloves on, enough of the poison had seeped through to react with his nervous system and basically shut him down. The six pallbearers listened closely to this report, as they realized how close they had been to experiencing the same fate. It would take the expertise of the entire medical team in Lyon to save the man's life, as well as months of rehabilitation. Together, they thanked Annette and Alan Cook for insisting they all wear the nitrile gloves under their cotton gloves.

As they were talking, another report was handed to Jacques. "It's just been confirmed . . . the guy in the hearse . . . the one than set up the cart thing . . . he was Ivan . . . Ivan the terrible from Russia. Because of what he was doing and the angles of the cameras, it took a little longer for the program to process those images . . . but yes, it's definitely him!"

"That does it then," said Jake,"It's only a matter of time . . . we hope . . .before that sonovabitch is put out of action!"

"We hope" repeated Jacques. He had hardly finished when somebody handed him another report. As Jacques read the report, a broad smile covered his face. Turning to the group he announced "Good news . . . actually bad news for Ivan . . . he was just picked up by the police . . . actually just outside the cemetery, he was in obvious distress and flagged down the police car and asked to be taken to the hospital." Jacques read some more. . . ."The officer recognized him from the bulletins we had sent out, and contacted headquarters . . . so nobody touched him until we had a hazmat team standing by. He must have slipped up when he was doctoring up those handles on the casket."

Jacques stopped reading and turned again to the group. "So . . . I think we can forget about Ivan the terrible as well as the Mistress of Murder. Maybe things can get 'back to normal' . . . whatever that is."

A round of applause broke out in the room, with smiles all around.

§

Jake turned to Matt and said " . . . 'back to normal' for you means back to dealing with drug cartels and more bad guys from the Balkans?"

Matt replied "Yes, I'm afraid so, but at least we won't have to be looking over our shoulder for these guys all the time."

Elena interrupted with "And . . . in case you guys would like to have a real holiday, relaxing, no threats of death and destruction . . . my parents have invited you back to the estancia for as long as you want . . . our guests."

Sabrina jumped at the chance. "Oh Jake! Why not? We loved it there, and would love to return."

Jacques overheard this exchange and added "Why not indeed? Go ahead you two, I'll try not to interrupt your little vacation with more bad guys to chase . . . and Jake, my friend, please take good care of my favourite law enforcement officer." as he smiled at Sabrina.

The End

CPSIA information can be obtained
at www.ICGtesting.com
Printed in the USA
LVHW022325020521
686271LV00016B/819